OUT OF THE SHADOWS

Newly single and enjoying her job as an office temp, Rowena Dexter sees new hope for the future when she starts dating barrister Tom Forrest. But memories of a terrifying child-hood incident resurface when she receives threatening e-mails. She was in the house when her aunt was murdered, and the case has never been solved. Rowena's former hus-band, Bruce, agrees to help her unmask the stalker, but can they solve the mystery before the mur-derer strikes again?

CATRIONA McCUAIG

♦

OUT OF THE SHADOWS

Complete and Unabridged

LINFORD
Leicester

First published in Great Britain in 2005

First Linford Edition
published 2007

Copyright © 2005 by Catriona McCuaig

British Library CIP Data

McCuaig, Catriona, *1938* –
    Out of the shadows.—Large print ed.—
Linford romance library
    1. Divorced women—Fiction
    2. Stalking—Fiction
    3. Romantic suspense novels
    4. Large type books
    I. Title
823.9′14 [F]

ISBN 978–1–84617–606–7

Published by
F. A. Thorpe (Publishing)
Anstey, Leicestershire

Set by Words & Graphics Ltd.
Anstey, Leicestershire
Printed and bound in Great Britain by
T. J. International Ltd., Padstow, Cornwall

This book is printed on acid-free paper

1

'Rat! Weasel!' Jude was quite red in the face with indignation. Rowena hid a smile. Her friend was so angry on her behalf and she did appreciate the support. Jude hadn't finished.

'After all you've done for him, giving up your good job at Harpers' to support him in his own venture, and now he has the nerve to leave you for some bimbo!'

The kettle was boiling. Rowena let her rant on while she made the tea, and by the time she brought it to the table Jude had run out of choice adjectives.

'So what will you do next? Sell this house, I suppose, and move away? I can't see you staying in the area when those two are living just streets away.'

'No, I don't see why I should be the one to move. I haven't done anything wrong. I'm going to stay put.'

And she hadn't done anything wrong. She had done everything possible to support her husband, Bruce Dexter, and it had come as a great shock to her when he had shamefacedly admitted to having an affair with a leggy young girl called Ariana, and added that he was moving in with her.

Bruce was an accountant, and when he decided to leave the firm he worked for to strike out on his own, Rowena had given him every encouragement. She had handed in her notice at Harpers' and gone to work with him at his new office, as secretary-cum-receptionist. Financially, it had been a struggle at first but she had every confidence that once they built up a clientèle things would get easier.

Bruce had landed a contract with a large company in the next town, going there at intervals to deal with tax matters, and it was there that he had met Ariana. While Rowena sat in the office, making out invoices and answering the phone, he had been taking

Ariana out to pub lunches and who knew what else.

'We went to see a solicitor, of course,' Rowena said, 'and she said we should divide up our assets so I get an equal share of everything.'

Jude nodded, reaching for another cherry tartlet.

'The trouble is, there isn't much to divide!' Rowena went on. 'The business isn't worth much at the moment, and even if it was awarded to me, it's nothing without Bruce, and of course we didn't own the building. So, he's staying put and living in the upstairs flat, and I get this house.'

Jude nodded approvingly. It was a very nice little house, in a quiet, tree-lined street, and it had a pretty little garden in the rear. Rowena felt a pang as she thought of that garden; she had once dreamed of a pram containing a rosy baby sitting in the shade of the lilac bushes.

She bit her lip.

'The thing is, Jude, there's a

3

mortgage to keep up. I'm not so sure I can do that on my own. I may have to sell, whether I like it or not.'

'Rubbish! With your qualifications you'll soon get a job, and if you didn't live here you'd have to pay rent somewhere, so what's the difference?'

What Jude said made sense, of course. If the house was sold at this stage it wouldn't leave Rowena with much of a nest egg. She had lain awake at night wondering how she was going to manage. Taking in a lodger or two was one option, but she didn't fancy having strangers in the house.

'There's nothing much advertised in the newspaper,' she said now, 'so I'll go down to the job centre on Monday and see what they have to offer.'

'You do that. And be sure to accept a post in some big office where there are lots of dishy men. The sooner you get back into the swing of things, the better!'

When her friend had gone, Rowena took a good look at herself in the mirror. The young woman who stared back at her would have been pretty if her big brown eyes hadn't looked so sad.

She pulled a wry face at herself. She couldn't go for interviews looking like this! She must book an appointment at the hairdresser.

Not for the first time she asked herself what Ariana had that she didn't. The girl was all legs and her style of dressing could be described as barely there. She had a flirtatious habit of tossing back her hair, and had a silly giggle Rowena thought would have driven Bruce mad. Obviously she didn't know him as well as she thought she did, after seven years of marriage.

Rowena was twenty-eight now, and Bruce thirty-five. Perhaps he was nearing the age when men needed to reassure themselves that they were still attractive to the opposite sex, or was it just that he had fallen into the clutches of a predatory woman and had been too flattered to resist?

In one way, Rowena hoped that he would tire of Ariana in time and come home with his tail between his legs, but if that happened, could she possibly forgive him? Surely nothing could ever be the same again.

In the meantime, she had to find work, and must make an effort to pick up the pieces of her shattered life. And that, as Jude had told her, meant that she had to become part of the dating scene again.

She had been shocked at that, reminding her friend that she was still married.

'Huh!' was Jude's response. 'You're separated, girl, soon to be divorced. Don't even think about sitting at home, licking your wounds. Get out there, and show the world you don't care!'

* * *

'Not much I can offer you, I'm afraid,' the brisk counsellor at the job centre sniffed. 'Supermarket shelf stacker, hospital auxiliary . . . '

'I have excellent computer skills,' Rowena pointed out, naming the software she was familiar with. 'I've been working for an accountant, and before that I was in the main office at Harpers'. I thought something along that line . . . '

The woman shrugged.

'Sorry! Nothing like that. Try again next week, why don't you.'

She glared at Rowena as if to say she mustn't want work too badly if she could afford to turn her nose up at the jobs on offer.

Rowena was dismissed. In need of comfort, she stepped into a nearby café and ordered coffee and a large slice of cheesecake. Keeping up the mortgage on one salary alone was going to be difficult; even with the most careful economies, the minimum wage would not allow for that.

'This seat taken?' A cheerful redhead plumped herself down without waiting for an answer. 'Saw you at the job centre, did I? Any luck?'

'No. I'm afraid not.'

'What you looking for, then?'

'Something in an office, I suppose. I didn't expect it was going to be so difficult. I have good computer skills so I was sure I'd be in demand.'

'Wish I did, but any kind of technology sends me all of a dither. Can't even programme the video,' the redhead announced, dumping a large amount of sugar into her mug of tea. 'Tell you what, though, you could go temping.'

'What?' Rowena wondered if she'd heard right.

'Temping. You know, every time somebody's off sick, or on maternity leave or something, they have to get a person to fill in until they come back. My cousin did that. She said it's a real hoot. You never get bored because it's something different every day. After a while she got offered a permanent job in one of the places she worked at, but she wouldn't take it. Freelancing was

8

more fun, see? There's a temp agency down Bridge Street. Why don't you give it a go?'

'Thanks very much, I will.'

★ ★ ★

The woman behind the desk was more encouraging than the lady at the job centre. She looked at Rowena's resumé with enthusiasm.

'Yes, very much sought after, especially as you're familiar with desktop publishing programmes as well as ordinary word processing. I'd be happy to have you sign on with us.'

And so she should be, Rowena thought ruefully, after learning about the rather stiff commission which was deducted off the top by the agency. Still, it would be worth it to find work which might not be advertised in any other way, and, who knew?

Leaving the agency in a more cheerful frame of mind, she went home, stopping to buy a few bits and pieces for her evening meal.

Optimistic by nature, Rowena felt sure that her luck was about to change. She was young, and enjoyed good health, and the world was her oyster.

It was not until she reached home and was inserting her key in the lock that the familiar feeling of dread came over her. As soon as Bruce had announced his intention of leaving she had had bolts installed on the back and front doors, and of course there was a chain and a peephole on the front door as well. Nevertheless, she still felt unsafe, living alone.

As soon as she had put her shopping down on the kitchen counter she made a quick tour of the house, making sure that everything was as she had left it. She peered inside the fitted wardrobe and even looked inside the airing cupboard, which was too small for even an elf to crawl into. Satisfied, she went to put the food away.

She remembered some work mates giggling about an older, single colleague who had mentioned how she always searched the house when she got home in case someone had broken in, and was still inside. Rowena hadn't laughed. But then Rowena's aunt had been murdered in her own home all those years ago, supposedly after surprising an intruder, although nothing had been taken.

The official conclusion was that person or persons unknown had entered the house, killed her when she caught them in the act of stealing her valuables and had then fled without stopping to collect the loot. The killer was never found, and Rowena supposed that the case had long ago been closed.

The trouble was, it could never be closed in Rowena's mind, because she had been there when it happened. Her parents had gone away for the weekend, celebrating their fifth wedding anniversary, leaving their three-year-old daughter in the care of her aunt, Bettina Nichols. Woken up by a noise and wanting a drink, the toddler had climbed out of bed and come to the head of the stairs, calling for her aunt.

Mercifully she hadn't gone downstairs but when Bettina failed to appear she had gone back to bed, howling, and after a while the neighbours from the adjoining semi, alarmed by the screams and thuds they'd heard through the wall, called the police.

Rowena had no actual memory of what had happened that night but of course her parents had told her about it when she was older. Now she was nervous about being alone in the house, although whether this was because she knew the story, or had some remaining trauma from the night of that long-ago crime, she had no idea.

She had always felt safe while Bruce was in the house, but he was gone now, and he probably wasn't coming back. Perhaps she should get a dog. A large one!

2

Rowena's first assignment was at a very nice bookstore, where she was greeted by the elderly owner with great relief.

'I'm told you can manage computers,' he said, before she could get her coat off. 'My daughter, Karen, usually deals with all that but she isn't here today. Gone to a schoolfriend's wedding and won't be back until tomorrow. I'm lost without her, and longing for the good old days when everything was down on paper.'

'I'm sure I can soon work out the system,' Rowena assured him. 'Why don't you go and put the kettle on while I boot up?' Anything to stop him breathing down her neck while she found her way around.

It was evident at once that Karen knew what she was doing, and fortunately Rowena was familiar with all the software she used, including an accounting programme favoured by Bruce.

Mr Anderson — her boss for the day — recovered his aplomb while demonstrating the procedure for dealing with credit card sales, obviously glad that Rowena didn't know everything.

They got on well together and by the time lunch time came he was ready to leave her in charge while he popped out to the nearby sandwich bar to have his midday meal. Rowena remained at the counter, keeping a wary eye on the customers.

Mr Anderson had explained that leaving them to browse was all part of the trade; people didn't want assistants leaping forward to ask if they could help. At the same time, shoplifting was to be avoided at all costs, but nobody could be accused of that unless they actually left the premises without paying.

'If you stop them inside the shop they could always say they meant to pay, or simply forgot,' he explained, 'and heaven knows it's easy enough to do. I'm always going upstairs to fetch something and when I get there I have no idea what it was I wanted. We do get some people who take advantage, of course. Just use your own judgement, Mrs Dexter.'

Momentarily distracted by a long-winded woman who wanted to buy a new book she'd seen advertised — although she couldn't remember the title or the author's name — Rowena didn't see the young man in the raincoat enter the shop.

When she next looked up it was to see him furtively shoving paperbacks into an inside pocket of his open raincoat.

Excusing herself, she strode over to the thief, amazed at her own daring.

'I'll take those, sir, and run them through for you. Will that be cash, or credit card?'

He pushed past her and made a rush for the door, with Rowena close behind. A male customer on the way in blocked the exit, grabbing the offender by the lapels. Rowena reached into the pocket and removed the books seconds before the man wriggled free and dashed across the street.

'Rowena!'

'Bruce!'

The pair looked at each other in amazement. Rowena felt her heart thumping. If she had ever had any doubt that she still loved her husband, they were stilled by this unexpected meeting. The way his eyes crinkled when he smiled, the little tuft of hair that always refused to lie down when he combed it, the blue striped shirt which she had laundered so often, all seemed inexpressibly dear.

'You're working here, Rowena? I'm shocked. I wouldn't have thought this would be your cup of tea.'

Rowena was annoyed. She had always enjoyed reading and would have liked nothing better than to work here permanently if only it was better paid. It was a charming little shop. How dare

Bruce come here insinuating that it was somehow too downmarket for his abandoned wife?

'I don't see what it has to do with you,' she said stiffly. 'In case it's escaped your notice, you left me with no means of support, so I have to work!' She wasn't about to tell him that she was working as a temp.

'Was there something you wanted, Bruce? Or were you just passing by and stopped to play the good Samaritan?'

'Um, I just wanted to know if the books I ordered were in yet.'

'I'll go and check.'

'No, no, I'll stop in another time. Ariana doesn't like it if I'm away from the office too long.'

'Too bad,' Rowena said to his retreating back.

She had forgotten about the lady at the counter, and hastened to apologise.

'Oh, don't mind me, dear. I thought it was perfectly splendid the way you stopped that young thief. If it was me, I'd have let him get away with it. You shouldn't have risked getting hurt, all for the sake of a few pounds' worth of crime novels. Still, you couldn't have done it without that other gentleman. A real Sir Galahad.'

'That was no gentleman, that was my husband,' Rowena remarked, in a parody of the old chestnut.

The old lady opened her eyes wide.

'Oh, my, but weren't you a bit stiff with him, dear? You see, if a woman wants to keep the romance in marriage, she has to make more of an effort, don't you think? May I suggest you read some of those lovely books by Barbara Cartland? Such an inspiration, I think you'll find.'

Rowena smiled through gritted teeth. She noticed that the customer wasn't wearing a wedding ring so probably she hadn't been married. What would she think if Rowena told her exactly what sort of Sir Galahad Bruce Dexter actually was? Better to leave that unsaid. The poor old soul had come here for a dose of romance, not to have

18

her cherished illusions shattered.

Mr Anderson returned from lunch, much refreshed.

'Your turn now, Mrs Dexter. The sandwich bar has some lovely broccoli soup today. I can recommend it.'

Smiling, Rowena retrieved her bag from under the counter and went out into the sunshine. She looked from left to right in the hope of seeing Bruce, but he had disappeared. Her appetite had gone so she went for a walk instead of stopping to eat; she would make a cup of tea when she went back to work.

Striding along in a daze she was shocked to find herself approaching Bruce's office without meaning to go in that direction. Really, she was like a lovesick schoolgirl, hanging around in the hope of engineering an accidental meeting with a boy! What if Ariana should be looking out of the window and happened to see her? How humiliating that would be! She would tell Bruce, and Rowena could imagine them laughing together at her expense.

She hurried back the way she had come. She simply had to stop grieving over Bruce. Jude kept inviting her to go dancing but that wasn't Rowena's style. Her way of coping was to throw herself into work, and if all the jobs that came her way were as pleasant as today's stint at the bookshop, that shouldn't be difficult.

3

After a week of temp work, Rowena found that she was thoroughly enjoying herself. After the bookshop she found herself wearing a white overall, sitting at the reception desk of a busy medical practice.

On reporting for work on the first day she had been given a lecture on medical ethics by the senior partner, a large, red-faced man with a harried expression.

'It is absolutely essential that you do not, at any time, pass on any information you may learn about while you are working here, Mrs Dexter,' he told her.

Rowena nodded. She hadn't needed the warning, of course, but he went on to underline the point.

'Occasionally a patient will ask for information concerning his own condition, Mrs Dexter. While you may have this at your fingertips, it is your job to refer him to his own doctor. Similarly, you must never give advice to patients. Is that clearly understood?'

'Yes, Doctor.'

It was just like being back at school, Rowena thought.

She was there for three days, replacing the receptionist who was off with flu. Greeting new arrivals, answering the phone and entering data into the computer kept her busy, and on her last morning she was surprised to find that she hadn't thought about Bruce for some time.

No work came her way for the rest of the week, and she was able to catch up on some household chores. Then, on Monday morning, she received an urgent call from the agency, asking her to report to a large law firm for the day. Someone had called in sick at the last moment and a replacement had to be found at once.

The chambers to which she was sent were situated in a large, Victorian house in the foregate. There was nobody at the desk when she went inside; probably it was the receptionist who was ill.

A tall, silver-haired man emerged from a nearby room and stopped short when he saw Rowena. Did she imagine it, or did a flicker of alarm or distaste cross his face momentarily? Her hand went up to her head automatically. Perhaps she looked a fright; a stiff breeze was blowing outside.

'Um, I'm Mrs Dexter,' she stammered. 'The temp,' she added, when there was no reply. 'I believe you sent for me?'

The distinguished-looking man found his voice.

'I'm sorry, I don't work here. Perhaps someone will attend to you in a moment.' He brushed past her, letting the main door slam shut behind him.

'Well!' Rowena was taken aback at his rudeness.

She peered at herself in the glass of a framed portrait but could see nothing wrong with her appearance.

'Oh, sorry, were you waiting for me?' The girl who spoke was plump and smiling, her hair highlighted with amazing blue streaks.

'I'm Mrs Dexter, the temp,' Rowena repeated.

'Oh, good. Come this way, and I'll take you to see Mr Forrest.'

'Who is he?'

'One of the barristers, and head of chambers. He said he wanted to speak to you first, and then I can show you the ropes. You're here to replace Maggie.'

'I hope she hasn't got this wretched flu that's doing the rounds.'

'Oh, no. Just morning sickness. Some days it's worse than others, I think.' She giggled.

★ ★ ★

A feeling like a small electric current went through Rowena when Mr Forrest got up to greet her, hand outstretched.

It wasn't simply that he was quite the most handsome man she had ever set eyes on, but she felt an instant attraction to him. Stupidly, she found herself wondering if he was married.

She gave herself a mental shake. Even if this black-haired, blue-eyed Adonis was single, he probably had dozens of women on his string and wouldn't know how to be faithful if he tried!

'Tom Forrest, Mrs Dexter. I'm glad you could come so promptly. We're in rather a muddle here today, as you'll find out. The work isn't very exciting, I'm afraid, mostly putting notes into the computer, but there's rather a backlog because Maggie hasn't been too well lately.'

As he had said, the work was fairly basic, and as Rowena's hands flew over the keyboard the pile of papers in Maggie's in-tray became smaller.

During coffee break she sat with Pauline, the receptionist who, without being asked, relayed all the office gossip. Rowena wondered if Mr Forrest had ever given her the confidentiality pep talk, but then maybe the girl didn't repeat any of this outside the office.

It turned out that Mr Forrest, Tom, was still single, although, as Rowena had surmised, he had more than his fair share of eager girlfriends.

'Is there anyone special at the moment?' she asked.

Pauline gave her a sly look.

'Interested, are we? There is one woman, a solicitor, who pops in to see him quite often, but that could be professional, I suppose.'

Rowena laughed and said, 'You have to admit, he is quite dishy!'

'Not my type, unfortunately. Not that he'd look at me if he was. To our Mr Forrest, I'm just the office dogsbody. Now you . . . ' She tilted her head to look appraisingly at Rowena. 'You could be quite something if you made a bit more of an effort.'

Rowena didn't know if she should take this as a compliment or an insult, but Pauline was blundering on, 'All I can say is, just you watch out. A love 'em and leave 'em type, that's what he is. 'Course, the woman who finally ropes him in will be sitting pretty, won't she?'

'I imagine barristers do make a lot of money,' Rowena murmured, at which Pauline gave a hoot of laughter.

'Oh, Mr Forrest doesn't have to make money, love. He's rolling in it. You should see his family home, a real mansion! Long, sweeping driveway, huge lawns, ornamental fountain, the lot!'

Rowena frowned and said, 'I don't recall a place like that round here.'

'Oh, it's outside Larchester. His mother lives there still but he has a flat here. One of those in that fancy new development on the Barton Road.'

'Then how do you know about this stately home, or whatever it is?'

'Staff outing, last year. The firm hired a mini bus and we all went there and had a barbeque on the terrace. Gosh, look at the time! Better get started if we still want jobs this time tomorrow!'

Rowena was about to leave the office at the end of the day when Pauline appeared at her side.

'Forrest wants you,' she said, jerking her thumb in the direction of the great man's door.

Wondering what was up, Rowena hurried over, hoping that he hadn't found fault with her work. She need not have worried.

'Do sit down, Mrs Dexter. The thing is, I've had a call from Maggie, and it seems she won't be back for some time to come.'

Rowena made the appropriate noises.

'The point is, Mrs Dexter, that she has to give up work immediately. How would you feel about taking her place for the next few months? It won't be a permanent position because, of course, we have to keep the job open for Maggie when the baby is old enough to be left, but it would offer you more security than this temp work you're doing at present.'

'I'd like that very much,' Rowena said, delighted, and was rewarded with a smile which made her go weak at the knees.

Tom Forrest had the knack of making a woman feel that she was the only person in the world who mattered to him. Not a feeling to be trusted, of course, in view of what Pauline had told her.

He pushed a set of forms over the desk towards her.

'Then would you like to fill these out? Personnel records. We'll need your details for tax deductions and so on.' He got up and left the room.

Rowena obediently filled in the usual details, date of birth, maiden name, marital status. With a pang, she ticked the box marked **Separated**.

'There's a phone call for you, Rowena. Take it in here if you like. I'll put it through.' This was Pauline, with her coat on. Another few minutes and the office would have been shut down for the day.

'Hello?'

'Oh, Mrs Dexter! I'm so glad I caught you. It's Edith Benson at the agency. This is rather urgent. I've another job for you, starting tomorrow, if you can take it on.'

Rowena's heart sank. She had been warned that temp work was either feast or famine and now she was being offered more than she could cope with.

'I'm sorry, Miss Benson. I've been offered a position here, while one of the employees is on maternity leave. I meant to let you know, of course, but the fact is that I knew nothing about it until a few moments ago. Once the job comes to an end, I'll sign on with you again, of course.'

'Oh, dear, I did hope . . . '

'What was this urgent job, then? Anything interesting?'

'Well, yes. It's Mr Evans, a very good customer. Morgan Evans, the writer, you know.'

Rowena did know. Not that she read his books; she didn't enjoy science fiction. However, in the brief time she had been at the bookshop she had seen how popular they were.

'The thing is, he insists on using an old-fashioned typewriter, added to which his manuscripts are an appalling mess, scrawled over with corrections and coffee stains. We always send one of our ladies to make a better copy, and as his publishers always request a disk to go with it, it has to be done on a computer, of course.

'Unfortunately, Sally, that's her name, is about to go to Florida with her husband, and isn't available. I'm afraid that Mr Evans is kicking up a terrible fuss. You were my last hope, Mrs Dexter.'

There was a pause, and then Rowena said slowly, 'Would I have to go to his home to do this work? I have my laptop at home, and if Mr Evans would let me take the manuscript away, I could work on it during the evenings and still keep my job here.'

Squawks of joy travelled over the telephone line. Rowena left the office feeling gleeful. It would mean intensive work for a while, but then what else did she have to do with her evenings, now that Bruce was gone? And the money would be very useful indeed.

Long afterwards she was to look back on this moment wishing she had turned these jobs down, but then how was she to know the dangers that lay ahead?

4

Morgan Evans lived in a charming old cottage on the Larchester Road. At least, it would have been delightful if the smell of burning had not greeted her as soon as the author ushered her inside. She couldn't help wrinkling her nose and he looked at her keenly as they shook hands.

'Baked beans, I'm afraid. I sat down at the typewriter while I put them on to heat and then I got carried away. I do hope the saucepan isn't ruined, or I shall have to buy another. Perhaps you can begin by cleaning it up?'

Rowena spoke firmly.

'I'm sorry, Mr Evans. I'm only here to pick up your manuscript for typing.'

He turned beetroot red.

'Oh, dear, have I made a mistake? I thought you must be the new cleaner. I asked the agency to find me one, you see, when I telephoned to request a replacement for Sally.'

Rowena took pity on him.

'I'll just have a look at the pan,' she said, 'but only to pass judgement, mind. And then you can show me the manuscript and I'll be on my way.'

Relieved, he showed her into the tiny kitchen, where the saucepan was sitting in the sink. He hadn't even put it to soak, she noted with some exasperation.

'Throw out these beans,' she instructed, 'and then pour some vinegar into the pan and leave it there. It may help to loosen the burnt bits on the bottom. And in future, leave things to soak in water if you haven't time to wash up immediately after a meal.'

Really, she sounded like an old-fashioned schoolmarm, she thought, grimacing at the pile of dirty plates that littered the draining board.

'Thank you, I'll try that,' he murmured, peering at the encrusted beans, but making no move to do anything about them.

Oh, well, it wasn't her problem, but she pitied the cleaning lady who would have to deal with all this.

Rowena followed the little man into his study, which was in even more of a mess than the kitchen. His typewriter, which was of the sit-up-and-beg variety, sat on a long table which was half hidden under a pile of papers. Cardboard boxes were stacked on the floor, and floor-to-ceiling shelves overflowed with books. The only tidy area of the room was a shelf holding the author's own books.

'Yes, those are mine,' he admitted, following her gaze.

There were hard-covered books with bright dust jackets, and paperbacks which seemed to have been published in a variety of foreign languages.

'You must be very proud of your work,' Rowena told him and he grinned at her, his eyes twinkling behind his thick glasses.

'I don't know about that, Mrs — er — Dexter, is it? When I'm writing

35

them, I'm happy enough, but each time I come to the end of a book I have my doubts. Will my editor like it? Will anyone want to buy it, and so on.'

Rowena knew that he fell into the fortunate category of authors whose readers bought the books sight unseen. It was refreshing to meet a successful person who lacked vanity.

'I mustn't keep you when you're so busy,' she told him, 'so if the manuscript is ready, I'll leave you to it.'

Turning to the table, he scrabbled around in the pile of papers and gathered up a large bundle, which he proceeded to push into a plastic supermarket bag before turning aside to search for a few more stray pages.

Horrified, Rowena watched him do this.

'Um, do you have a copy of all that?'

He raised his eyes to the ceiling.

'Mrs Dexter, I have two carbon copies. That's the first rule of writing books. Never let your only copy go out of your hands. I should have thought that even a computer typist would have known that.'

So the absent-minded professor persona did not extend to his professional life. Even so, Rowena resolved to go straight home. She would not feel comfortable until the manuscript was safely under lock and key.

All business now, Morgan Evans told her what was expected of her.

'I want you to type out everything exactly as I have written it. You are not to change anything, Mrs Dexter, anything at all, even if you feel I should have worded something differently. Any changes that have to be made will be suggested by my editor, not by you. Do you understand?'

She nodded dutifully.

'But what about errors, Mr Evans? Obvious spelling mistakes? Do I leave those in?'

He hesitated.

'All right, I suppose you may tidy those up, but, mind, I shall read the finished typescript most carefully. If I find you have made mistakes of your own I shall request corrections, at your own expense!'

Chastened, Rowena took her leave, wondering if she might have bitten off more than she could chew. She was rather glad that she had Miss Benson to act as go-between in this case.

Rowena looked forward to going to work each day at the chambers of Forrest, Dean & Schroeder. Jennifer Dean was a smart, thirty-something barrister who didn't suffer fools gladly, yet she was pleasant enough to Rowena and always polite when she gave her work to do.

Striding around in her severe business suit and expensive high-heeled shoes she appeared extremely capable and it was no wonder that she had been made a partner at such a young age. Rowena wondered if she and Tom Forrest were anything more than professional associates, but in the office at least they seemed to be intent on their own work.

Pauline sauntered by Rowena's desk on her way to the copier.

'Forrest is back,' she hissed, out of the side of her mouth. 'Court's over early.'

But Rowena wasn't slacking off, so hadn't needed the warning. Frowning at the computer screen she wasn't aware that he had come to stand beside her until he spoke.

'Everything going well, Mrs Dexter?'

'Yes, thank you, Mr Forrest.'

'Isn't it time you started calling me Tom? And I'm sure you won't mind if I call you Rowena.'

She looked up at those blue eyes and felt a quiver in her stomach. She nodded, not trusting herself to speak.

'I'm just off to lunch,' he announced. 'Perhaps you'd like to come with me?'

'Oh, I've brought a sandwich from home,' she told him.

It was one thing to feel attracted to him but quite another to be added to his string of conquests, if that was what he had in mind. Pauline had warned her that he had a careless way with women, and after Bruce had left her for Ariana, Rowena had lost confidence. Why would the handsome and wealthy Tom Forrest be interested in her?

But perhaps he wasn't, for he went on to say, 'Do come, I'm hungry enough to eat a bear. And I want to talk to you anyway, about work. Never mind the sandwich. We'll walk back through the park and you can feed it to the ducks. Now, what do you say?'

'I don't think the ducks would like cheese and chutney.' She smiled, but she stood up and reached for her handbag.

Over a prawn and avocado salad, followed by roast chicken, Tom asked polite questions about her background.

'I noticed in your personnel file that you're separated from your husband,' he said, pouring more white wine into her glass. 'Is that a recent occurrence?'

Her heart gave a painful thump but she managed to answer calmly.

'Yes, not long ago. My husband

found somebody more to his liking, I'm afraid.'

'More fool him,' Tom said, patting her hand sympathetically. She withdrew it and picked up her fork. 'I hope you plan to take him for all you can get. I can recommend a good solicitor, if you like.'

'Not much point in that, I'm afraid. We both gave up our jobs a year ago so that Bruce could start his own firm. I'm sure it will be a success, given time, but at this point it hasn't really taken off, so there are few assets to be divided, from the firm, that is. He gets that, and I have our house, mortgage and all.'

'Then your husband is even more of a fool than I thought. I hope this girl is worth it.'

Seeing Rowena's miserable expression, he adroitly changed the subject.

'About work. The thing is, we're about to get the painters and decorators in. The office is going to be in a bit of a mess for the next few weeks and there won't be room to swing a cat.'

Rowena's heart sank. Was she about to get the sack?

'So I was wondering,' he went on, 'do you have a computer at home? And are you online?'

'Yes, to both questions.'

'Then how would you like to work out of your home for the next little while? There are a lot of old files we want to transfer to the computer because they take up so much space in hard copy. Having it all on computer will make it so much quicker to look things up as well.

'Naturally there's more to this work than simple word processing, but you have the required experience with the software we'd be using and it would be child's play for you. You could come to the office once a week and transfer everything into the system. What do you think?'

Rowena was delighted. She quickly negotiated the terms of this new work. Tom agreed that, as she was working in her own home, there was no need for her to keep office hours, or to take the usual breaks.

'If you want to down tools to go out shopping or something, that would be fine,' he said. 'This will be tedious work, I'm sure, and if you sit at it for hours on end, you could make annoying errors.'

'Do I keep an account of my hours, then?'

He shook his head.

'No need for that. I'm sure I can depend on you to give us our money's worth!'

Rowena nodded happily. She could alternate the work with inputting Morgan Evans' manuscript and she would prepare nutritious dinners to cook while she was on the job. There would be no more coming home exhausted after a day at the office, too tired to cook a proper meal and settling for a sandwich. It had been different when there was Bruce to consider, but for one person it seemed too much of an effort.

'You don't have a car, do you?'

She came to with a start to realise that Tom was saying something.

'Er, sorry, I was miles away.'

'A car. I said, you don't have a car, do you? You won't be able to manage all those boxes of files on the bus, so I'll run them over for you and pick them up when you've finished.'

That was another sore point. Rowena could drive, of course, but she and Bruce had only been able to afford one car. Anyway, they hadn't needed two, because they worked together. When they split up she automatically agreed that Bruce should keep the vehicle, because he had to make numerous trips out of town in connection with the job.

Now she wondered why she had been such a doormat. She was not receiving financial support from Bruce so she had to work for her living, and having the car might have given her a wider choice of employment.

* * *

44

That evening, Rowena made a start on Morgan Evans' manuscript. As Miss Benson had said, it was a mess. Rather than giving her the original he had supplied her with a carbon copy, but some of the corrections he had scrawled on the original hadn't come through properly and she was obliged to peer at them through a magnifying glass to try to make them out.

No wonder his publisher wanted the work on disk. She was beginning to wish that she had asked to be paid by the hour rather than by the completed job!

Rowena was not a fan of science fiction novels. However, Morgan Evans obviously knew what he was doing, and, caught up in the plot, she worked quickly, her fingers flying over the keyboard.

She came to a stop, puzzled, when she realised that she had just typed something similar on a previous page. A whole scenario seemed to be played out twice, with slight variations. Was this meant to be, or had Mr Evans given her two separate drafts by mistake? He had insisted that she was not to make any amendments, yet should she let this slip by?

No doubt his editor would catch the mistake, if indeed it was one, but then Rowena might have to go through the material a second time, at her own expense, and she certainly didn't want that. Further along there was a section where the hero, Rangi, played a major part, but, surely, that should have been Radu?

Thoroughly confused by now, Rowena realised that she had to speak to Mr Evans before going on. It was a lovely evening. She might as well go over to his cottage and ask him to explain.

The smell at the cottage when she arrived was worse than before.

'Been burning the beans again?' she joked, hoping to raise a smile before telling him why she had turned up on his doorstep. He glared at her.

'Kettle boiled dry. Burned the bottom

out. The handle is still good, though.'

Was this an attempt at a joke? Apparently not; he was still scowling. She fared no better when she explained her problem with his manuscript.

'Think you're a critic, do you? May I remind you that you're being paid to reproduce the work as is?'

Swallowing a curt reply, Rowena fumbled through the papers and produced the offending pages. He grudgingly agreed that she was right and made the corrections with great slashing strokes of a red pen.

'Now, was there anything else? If not, you must allow me to get on. I was in the middle of a crucial development before that stupid kettle ran amok.'

Rowena found herself outside, with the door closed firmly behind her. Charming! Anyone would think it was all her fault. And what was he working on now? She sincerely hoped it was a new book, and not some major plot changes to the one she was busily typing up!

By the time she reached home it was getting late and she decided to have an early night, resuming work in the morning. She might just check her e-mails first, though. There might be something from her parents, who now lived in Australia.

Sure enough, there was one from her mother, anxiously asking how she was getting along, and suggesting that now was the time to think about a holiday down under.

Rowena composed a cheerful reply, saying little about her emotional state, but making an amusing story out of her visit to Morgan Evans' cottage. It was when she was about to close down the computer for the night that the new e-mail came in.

People who don't mind their own business could be in deadly danger, it said. *Remember this and be warned.*

Shaken, she deleted the message at once. She tried to tell herself that she was being ridiculous. It was probably from some teenage boy who had nothing better to do than send stupid messages to women.

But the message kept going round and round in her head and it was a long time before she was able to fall asleep.

5

It was around this time that Rowena had a falling out with Jude. They had been friends since their school days, cycling and playing tennis in the summer and going to the roller skating rink in winter. They had laughed and cried over their various youthful romances, and discussed their hopes and dreams for the future.

Rowena had been Jude's bridesmaid when her friend embarked on a short-lived marriage, and Jude had returned the honour for Rowena. She had been an unfailing support when Bruce walked away from his obligations in search of what he thought was something better.

Both women had been unlucky enough to choose men who let them down, but there the resemblance had ended. Jude had become very bitter after finding out that Keith had had a string of affairs, almost from day one.

'I've had it with marriage!' she told Rowena, over and over again. 'I did my best to be a good wife to him, and for what? All that cooking and cleaning, picking up after the brute and dispensing sympathy when he didn't get promotion at work. But was that enough for him? No. So from now on my motto is going to be use or be used.'

Rowena, on the other hand, still had faith in romance. There were plenty of single men out there; they couldn't be all bad eggs. She had made one false start, that was all. There was still time to find someone wonderful, someone with whom to live happily ever after.

Underneath it all, she still yearned after Bruce. She fantasised that he would tire of Ariana and would return, begging to be taken back. But if that were to happen, could she forgive and forget?

When she thought of the younger woman in Bruce's arms, it made her want to scream.

Jude showed no sympathy when Rowena mentioned this.

'Good riddance to bad rubbish, I say. They deserve each other. You have to move on. Find yourself another man, as I have.'

Since the break-up of her marriage, Jude had dated a string of men, all of whom, according to her, had some fatal flaw. Rowena secretly thought that Jude's newly-abrasive manner might be frightening them off, but there was no way she was going to say so.

'Patsy and I are going to that new singles' club that's opened up on Wynd Street,' Jude told her. 'Why don't you come along? We'll have a few laughs.'

Rowena shook her head.

'No thanks, it's not really my scene.'

'How do you know, until you try it?'

But Rowena was still feeling fragile after Bruce's defection and the thought of getting into the dating scene so soon was too much to contemplate.

'Well, are you coming with us, or not?'

Rowena spoke without thinking.

'I don't think I'm ready to try picking up somebody in a bar, Jude. It just isn't me.' She could have bitten her tongue out, but it was too late.

Jude's expression hardened.

'You sound like my grandmother, Rowena. Nice girls don't pick up strange men, is that it? Well, for your information, we are not looking for a one-night stand. Singles' clubs are places where lonely people can meet members of the opposite sex. If it leads to a date, that's fine. If not, we've had a nice evening in pleasant company. That's all.'

'I didn't mean it like it sounded,' Rowena protested, blundering on. 'Some very nice people go to those places, I'm sure, but you hear such awful things on the news, don't you? Surely it's better to be safe than sorry.'

'Well, if that's how you feel, you certainly don't have to come along,

Miss Prim!' Jude snapped. 'Patsy and I will keep each other company.'

Almost in tears now, Rowena tried to set the matter right, but there was no reasoning with her friend, who stormed off with her head held high. She hadn't meant to hurt Jude's feelings, or to imply there was anything wrong with going to a club to make new friends. It was just that she knew herself too well.

She had lost confidence since being left by her husband, and she was intimidated by the thought of trying to make bright conversation with a stranger.

★　★　★

Tom arrived with an armload of boxes.

'This lot should keep you busy for a while,' he said. 'I wish I could move in here for the duration. The painters have moved into the office and you wouldn't believe the mess, never mind the fumes. Pauline is staggering around clutching a handkerchief to her nose, muttering something about wanting us to supply her with an industrial face mask.'

Rowena laughed.

'Is it really that bad? Surely they can't be working everywhere at once.'

'No, of course not. They're doing one room at a time, behind closed doors. It's just that we're having to double up, which is a bit of a nuisance. We wanted them to do the work during our annual holiday, but this was the only time they could come, so we just have to put up with it.'

He glanced at his watch.

'Time for lunch. What about coming out with me for soup and a sandwich?'

Rowena cast a doubtful glance at the pile of boxes.

'I should make a start on the work,' she told him, but he shook his head.

'Nonsense! Nothing there that can't wait. And I am the boss, remember!'

He grinned, and she needed no further persuading.

'I'll get my jacket,' she dimpled.

Tom asked for broccoli soup and a ham sandwich on wholewheat bread, while Rowena opted for mushroom quiche and a green salad. She was flattered when he told her about his latest case, defending a woman who had been caught shoplifting.

'Pretty small town stuff, of course, but it pays the rent,' he explained.

'Yes, I suppose rents are quite high in that part of town,' Rowena said, taking him seriously. He laughed.

'Just a figure of speech, of course. We do own the building.'

'Of course,' she echoed, feeling foolish.

As Pauline had told her, Tom came from a wealthy family, who had a beautiful estate in the country. She wished that she could see it. Perhaps there would be another company outing and she would be invited to attend.

As if he could read her mind, he began to talk about his home.

'I have to go out to the country this weekend,' he told her. 'It's Mother's and Dad's ruby wedding anniversary and we all have to be on deck.'

'That's forty years, isn't it?' Rowena mused. 'Quite an achievement, especially nowadays. You said all. That means you have brothers and sisters, I suppose?'

He pulled a face.

'Three sisters, all older than me, and quite a time I had of it, growing up, I can assure you. Bossy boots, all three of them. Still, it taught me how to deal with the opposite sex. These days they all want me to settle down, but so far I've managed to avoid any permanent attachments!'

He laughed, and Rowena began to feel more at ease with him. Pauline had indicated that he was a love 'em and leave 'em type, but he seemed a nice enough chap and possibly he hadn't yet found the right person with whom to spend the rest of his life.

'Anyway, I'm supposed to bring a date, so how about it, Rowena?'

'What?' She was momentarily confused.

'My parents' anniversary. Would you

like to come with me to the celebration?'

After a moment's hesitation, she accepted with pleasure, and he paid the bill and left, promising to collect her on Saturday morning. He had offered to give her a lift home, but she refused, saying she needed the exercise, and would walk. In reality, she needed time to think. She would never settle down to work if she sat down in this state.

What to wear? That was the problem. Normally she would have discussed this with Jude and they would have had a fine time touring the shops and trying on outrageous garments before selecting something suitable. That wasn't possible now. She was tempted to phone her friend, but was afraid of being snubbed. If she was still smouldering, Jude might say something about Rowena hobnobbing with the élite while lesser mortals had to rely on the singles' scene for companionship.

The problem was that money was tight. Her mortgage payment was due, and it seemed foolish to run up a credit card bill to buy a dress meant to impress people she would probably never meet again. She would have to make do with what she had.

The main event was to be a catered dinner at the Forrests' home, a sit down meal indoors, followed by dancing in a marquee on the lawn. The rest of the weekend was to be spent doing — what? Tom had been vague about this.

'Oh, you know, just lazing about.'

She hoped that Tom's sisters would be nice. He had explained that all three were married, and would be bringing their small children with them, so probably their offspring would keep them too busy for them to pay much attention to Rowena. Otherwise they might be sizing her up as a possible sister-in-law, which she could do without.

Oh, well, she would have to take things as they came. She would have a pleasant weekend and return refreshed, ready to tackle the work for which she was being paid. And speaking of work . . . She quickened her pace. She must get home and do a few more pages of Morgan Evans' manuscript.

It was hard going, but rather fun to be involved with the work of such a well-known author. She resolved that when the book came out she would buy a copy, as a souvenir. She might even get it autographed!

*　*　*

After listening to Pauline raving about Tom's home in the country, Rowena had imagined some huge mansion, rather like Brideshead in the television series. However, Courtneys, as it was called, was not a stately home but simply a very old and beautiful house, standing in its own grounds.

As Tom's car swept up the long drive between fields where sheep and horses grazed peacefully, he explained that it dated back to the eighteenth century, when it had been the home of a prosperous landowner. Tom's parents had bought it years before when the last descendant passed away at a great age.

'Of course, Mother and Dad had it modernised throughout,' he said. 'Wash stands with a jug and basin, and a receptacle under the bed may have been the latest thing in Victorian times but nobody would put up with that nowadays.'

Rowena wondered how a young married couple had been able to afford such a place, run down or not, but she didn't like to ask. Pauline had hinted that Mrs Forrest had come from a moneyed family so that must be the answer.

'I wonder how your parents manage the house,' she asked and hoped he wouldn't think she was prying.

'Oh, they have a couple of daily women who keep the place in order, and a gardener outside,' he said easily. 'When I was growing up we had a cook who lived in, but when she retired they decided not to replace her. Mother quite enjoys cooking, when the two of them are on their own, and even Dad has been known to scramble an egg or two. When they want to give a big bash they just call in the caterers. It's easier that way.'

Rowena agreed that it must be. How blissful to give a dinner party where you could sit down with your guests and be waited on hand and foot. Not like the occasional dinners she and Bruce had hosted for friends, where Rowena had spent half the time in the kitchen, putting the finishing touches on the meal while Bruce plied the guests with drinks and enjoyed their company. What sort of hostess would Ariana make? Rowena couldn't imagine her in a hot kitchen, basting the chicken.

A number of cars were drawn up in the forecourt.

'We're not late, are we?' Rowena was nervous enough about meeting Tom's people without starting off on the wrong foot.

'No, no. Just my sisters and their entourage. The guests won't arrive until this evening.'

'Uncle Tom! Uncle Tom!' As their car came to a halt, a cluster of young children rushed to the car, ignoring Rowena.

'Steady on, you'll have me over!' He gently removed himself from the clutches of a tow-headed toddler who was hanging on to his knees. 'Say how d'you do to Mrs Dexter.'

But with assorted shrieks they rushed off, pretending to be aeroplanes.

'As you may have guessed, those were my nephews and nieces.' He grinned.

'Goodness! How many are there?'

'The five you've just seen, and a couple of babies, who are inside, no doubt, being adored by their loving grandmother. Now, are you ready for the fray?'

The morning-room seemed to be full of women. Nell Forrest was petite, with carefully-waved hair. She was wearing a two-piece beige outfit in Irish linen,

63

with a colourful scarf at the neck. She greeted Rowena sweetly.

'You're very welcome, my dear. I'm always pleased to meet Tom's little friends.'

Rowena almost giggled. By the way this elegant lady spoke, she might have been an eight-year-old, coming over to play with the other children. Still, at least she hadn't been mistaken for a girlfriend, which could have been awkward.

Tom indicated his sisters, Deborah, Liz and Margaret. They all looked very much alike, with short, dark hair and grey eyes. They were all wearing simple but expensive-looking casual clothes. Rowena would have liked to know what their husbands did for a living to provide all those designer garments, but perhaps the women, too, had professions. It was hard to tell.

'You'll look after Rowena, won't you? We're going down to the pub for a bit.' Tom glanced at his watch. 'We have things to discuss. We'll be back in plenty of time for lunch.'

Apparently 'we' meant Tom and the husbands. Rowena felt annoyed at this casual treatment. Why wasn't she invited to go with them? She was here as Tom's guest, after all. But she smiled bravely and he strode off without a word of apology.

His three sisters continued their conversation, which was all about their children, and people Rowena didn't know. She sat back, grateful that she didn't have to join in. What could she have said?

She gathered that Deborah, the mother of three, had a professional nanny, who had come with them. This young woman was to take charge of all seven children while their parents joined in the celebrations.

'I hope it won't be too much for her, with the two babies,' Liz said. 'The first thing I'm going to do when we get home is give that useless au pair the sack. Of course I wanted her to come with us, and do you know what she said? Told me this was supposed to be her free weekend, and she didn't see why she should change. Really!'

'You're lucky to have anyone at all,' Margaret put in. 'If you had to manage alone, with a new baby and a two-year-old, you'd know what work really is.'

Her sisters had probably heard this complaint often enough before, because they didn't reply. Deborah turned to Rowena.

'I'm so sorry. Here we are, airing our silly little complaints, and ignoring you completely. You must think us very rude. Now, tell us all about yourself. How did you meet our baby brother?'

'We didn't meet, exactly,' Rowena mumbled. 'I'm working for the firm, temporarily, that is, while somebody is on maternity leave. Maggie, I think her name is.'

Deborah nodded. 'Oh, I see. And I suppose Jenny couldn't make it this weekend, so you're filling in once again.'

'Jenny?'

'Jennifer Dean, his partner in the firm. He brings her home from time to time.'

Rowena wondered why she suddenly felt so disappointed. So she was just here playing second fiddle, because Ms Dean was otherwise engaged that weekend. She also felt rather annoyed. If Tom did have some obligation to the attractive young barrister, should he be taking Rowena to lunch and to his parents' anniversary party? How would Ms Dean feel about it if she knew?

Rowena gave herself a mental shake. The couple were not living together so perhaps there wasn't much of a commitment between them as yet. And was she being over-sensitive because of her own experience with Ariana? Best take things at face value and enjoy this weekend, seeing how the other half lives, she decided.

Lunch was a casual affair of paté, assorted breads and fruit, accompanied by white wine. Mrs Forrest announced that she was going to spend the afternoon in bed.

'Someone can wake me up at four o'clock with a nice cup of tea,' she declared. 'I want to be full of energy for the evening ahead. I intend to dance into the small hours of the morning.'

Her husband groaned.

'You can count me out, then, or I'll be too tired for golf in the morning.'

There was a gale of laughter from his family. His wife shook her head in mock disapproval.

'You and your golf, John! You can give it a miss for once. It isn't every day that one celebrates a ruby wedding. You'll do as I tell you for once, and like it!'

Rowena's heart sank. Golf! She didn't play, of course. Bruce would have liked to try it but they hadn't been able to afford it. Would everybody go off to play, leaving her trotting miserably in their wake? But Tom came to her rescue.

'What would you like to do this afternoon, Rowena? How about tennis?

Or do you ride?'

Luckily, she was prepared to do either one. She had played tennis at school, and had been a horse-mad teenager, hiring mounts from a local stable whenever she could afford it.

'We'll go riding in the morning, then,' Tom said, 'when all these fanatics are away at the golf course. We'll have a game of tennis now, shall we, if you feel up to it?'

So they went to play on the hard court behind the house. Tom was much the better player and won every set, but Rowena acquitted herself fairly well and thoroughly enjoyed herself.

They strolled back to the house with Tom's arm draped carelessly over her shoulder and she realised that she hadn't given a thought to faithless Bruce all afternoon. Maybe she was beginning to come to terms with the situation.

Dinner was a formal affair. The dining-room was too small to accommodate so many guests, so long tables had been set up in the library, decorated in red, as befitted a ruby wedding celebration. They were covered with burgundy-coloured drapery underneath white tablecloths, and the floral decorations were made from dark red roses, which must have cost a bomb.

While the guests were standing around, drinks in hand, waiting for dinner to be announced, more people continued to arrive. There were shrieks of joy from Mrs Forrest when a tall, elegant woman came into the room. Tom explained to Rowena that all the original members of the bridal party were present for the occasion, including this Peggy Prentice, who had come all the way from Australia!

Rowena was introduced to many of the newcomers, although their names instantly went out of her head.

'And who is this lovely young lady?'

A tall, distinguished-looking man had come up behind them and Tom swung around with a welcoming smile on his face.

'Uncle Mark! This is my friend, Rowena Dexter. Rowena, I don't think you've met my uncle, Mark . . . '

But the surname was lost as he was pounced on by his sister, Margaret.

'You'll never guess who's here!' she enthused, dragging him away.

Tom looked back over his shoulder, laughing.

'Sorry about this, Rowena. Back in a minute!'

Mark regarded Rowena with a piercing look that seemed to go right through her. She felt uncomfortable with his scrutiny, without understanding why.

'Haven't we met before?'

She shook her head, then she remembered. Of course! This was the man she had spoken to on her first day at Tom's chambers. He had told her that he didn't work there. He had obviously called in to speak to his nephew.

She smiled.

'Yes, I do remember now. You were

the man who . . . '

But once again there was an interruption. One of the caterers was ringing a small hand bell, wanting their attention.

'Ladies and gentlemen, dinner is served. Would you take your places, please?'

Tom came over and took her arm.

'May I escort you to the table, madam?' he joked. Laughing, she turned back to apologise to Uncle Mark, but he was already striding towards the library. A strange man, Rowena thought. Perhaps he was shy.

After the meal, there was dancing. The glass doors stood open and the guests trooped over the terrace and on to the lawn, where the marquee was a hive of activity. Brightly-coloured lights twinkled in the trees, and the effect was magical.

Musicians were playing golden oldies, and there was clapping when Tom's father bowed to his wife and they took the floor together. The sight of Mrs Forrest smiling up at her husband gave Rowena a pang. What must it be like to have enjoyed forty years of a good marriage? She had once thought that she and Bruce would be together for ever.

She wasn't left moping on the sidelines for very long. Tom led her into the middle of the throng, and after she had returned to her seat his brothers-in-law each in turn requested a dance. Either they all had perfect manners or Tom's mother had had a word with them. Whichever it was, Rowena was grateful not to be languishing as a wallflower.

The gorgeous Ariana would have had the men lined up six deep, of course, and Jude would certainly not have been intimidated by her surroundings. She would probably have asked the nearest man to dance, whether or not it was a ladies' choice!

As the evening wore on, the band began to play music that was slower and more intimate. Tom took Rowena in his arms once more, holding her close, his lips brushing her hair. When they arrived at the entrance to the marquee he took her by the hand, and stepped out into the cool night air.

In a dream, she walked beside him to a tiny pool where a fountain played. He gave her a lingering kiss and she closed her eyes, savouring the moment.

'I'll wake up when the clock strikes twelve,' she told herself, 'and this will all be over.' But the evening had gone by in a flash, and it was already two o'clock.

★ ★ ★

After lunch the next day, Tom and Rowena left to return to town, after the usual thanks and goodbyes.

'Do come again,' Mrs Forrest told Rowena.

'Thank you, I'd love to,' she said, although whether she would be invited again was anybody's guess.

It didn't seem likely, if Tom had something going with Ms Dean; the kiss in the moonlight was probably just something that had happened on the spur of the moment. Still, it had been a delightful weekend. Rowena had felt desirable and happier than she had been in a long time.

'We must do this again,' Tom told her, when the car drew up in front of her house. He leaned over and kissed the top of her head.

'That would be lovely,' she said, heaving her weekend bag out of the back seat.

Later, throwing her things into the clothes hamper, she felt very much like Cinderella on the morning after the ball. Would Prince Charming come seeking her again? Only time would tell. Too restless to settle down to doing anything constructive she went to the computer.

With any luck there would be an e-mail from Mum in Australia. She would be interested to hear about Rowena's weekend, and glad that her daughter was getting out and about instead of glooming around at home.

The message that came up on the screen shocked and disturbed her.

You haven't been paying attention, have you? Get out now, while there's still time. Death comes to those who outstay their welcome.

6

The constable at the police station was sympathetic but unable to offer any help.

'This sort of thing happens all the time, miss. People with nothing better to do than send out these messages to all and sundry.'

'But I copied down the e-mail address of the person who sent it,' Rowena protested. 'Surely you can follow it up, and charge them with mischief, or something? At least warn them off.'

He shook his head.

'Whoever it is will have changed the address by now, and I advise you to do the same.'

'But I don't understand how this person got hold of my address in the first place. I mean, I don't have a website, I don't post messages on bulletin boards. There aren't many people who know what my address is.'

The constable shrugged.

'It's probably just a hit or miss thing. These people send out thousands of messages to many different combinations of names and numbers. It's just by chance that this one reached you.'

'But this is the second one I've had,' Rowena wailed.

'I'm very sorry, I'd like to help, but there really isn't anything we can do.'

He turned to a woman who had been waiting impatiently beside Rowena. She began a long tale of woe about a missing cat, and Rowena turned away, almost in tears.

She didn't believe for a moment that the messages had come to her by coincidence. The first part of her e-mail address was a made-up word from her childhood days, not something that a stranger would easily pick up on.

So who was trying to frighten her? At home, cradling a cup of steaming tea between her cold hands, she went over the possibilities. Her parents had her address, of course, but it wouldn't be them.

Jude? She was fed up with Rowena at the moment, but surely she wouldn't go this far? Bruce knew what it was. Could Ariana be playing tricks? And of course the address was on file at work, but why should anyone there do this?

For one wild moment Rowena considered Ms Dean, annoyed because Tom had taken her to his parents' anniversary celebrations, but then she laughed at herself. The self-confident barrister was unlikely to stoop so low, and in any case would be more aware than most people of the penalties attached to making threats to innocent people. So who could it be? Rowena racked her brains, but could come up with nothing.

* * *

Rowena kept busy over the next few weeks, working all hours to keep her mind off the problem of the unpleasant e-mails. She went to the office once a week to transfer the files on to the main computer, and from time to time Tom turned up with more boxes of documents.

'I appreciate your work,' Tom assured her. 'And to prove it, I'll take you to lunch!'

This became a regular occurrence until Rowena began to think that she knew Tom quite well. They might come from different worlds but nevertheless they seemed to have a lot in common. When he invited her to a concert at the town hall she didn't hesitate. Suddenly they seemed to be an item.

She also completed the retyping of Morgan Evans' manuscript and delivered it to his home. He examined it carefully and grudgingly admitted that she had done a good job.

'You can do this lot, when I get it finished,' he told her, indicating an untidy pile of papers beside his typewriter. 'You won't let the temp agency know about our arrangement, I trust. Between the fifteen per cent I have to pay my agent, and what the agency charges, it's a wonder I can make a living at all. If we can cut out the middleman, so much the better!'

Rowena decided that this was exaggeration. Surely the agency's commission came out of her wages, not his payment to them? And she didn't want to risk being crossed off Miss Benson's books.

'We'll have to see,' she murmured, resolving that if he did give her the job she would insist on working from his original copy, not the smudged carbons.

She had just reached home when the doorbell rang. Nervously peering through the spy hole she recognised Bruce, and flung the door open to let him in.

'You took long enough to answer,' he grumbled. 'Anybody might have seen me standing here!'

'Are the police after you, then?' she asked lightly, standing aside to let him pass. He looked indignant.

'Of course not.'

'Well, then, why should it matter if anyone saw you on your wife's door-step?'

'Oh, well, you know.'

She thought that she did. Perhaps Ariana was jealous. After all, if Bruce had left his wife for her, it was always possible that his new love would in turn be left for someone else, as the roving male looked around in search of pastures new. Well, let her suffer!

'I was just about to make lunch. Would you like some?'

He sat at the kitchen table, watching Rowena as she made grilled cheese sandwiches and opened a tin of vegetable soup. She made celery sticks for herself but didn't offer any to Bruce, who always referred to this healthy snack as rabbit food.

'So, how's the business going?' she asked, when they were enjoying their meal.

Bruce grimaced.

'Slowly, I'm afraid. I keep hoping that

things will pick up but I haven't managed to land any new clients in a while.'

This was his cue to ask Rowena how she was getting along, where she was working and so on, but he seemed too wrapped up in his own troubles to get into that.

'Half the problem is not having anyone in the office to depend on,' he continued. 'Either I have to drop everything to answer the phone, or I miss calls altogether when I'm out in the field. It doesn't make for maximum efficiency.'

'But what about Ariana? I understood from what you said before that she is working with you in the business.'

He shrugged.

'Supposed to be, but she's hardly ever there. She always seems to have something urgent she wants to do, shopping or meeting a friend.'

Rowena murmured something noncommittal. On one hand she was secretly pleased that Ariana was showing her true colours and making Bruce realise that she was less than perfect, but on the other, this was the man Rowena still loved, and she hated to see him suffer.

'She just doesn't understand my position,' he complained, crumbling his sandwich. 'The thing is, she doesn't really need to work at the moment because her great aunt died and left her a small legacy. When I remind her of our agreement, that she should help me in the office, she tells me to bring in a temp.'

He looked up at Rowena as if a light bulb had just come on over his head.

'I don't suppose you'd like to . . . '

'I certainly would not!' she scoffed. 'Honestly, Bruce. What do you think I am, some kind of idiot? You leave me for that floozy and then you expect me to come back to help you out, when you're still living with her? And may I remind you that when I was working there I did it for free, because I was doing it for us. Yes, I work as a temp now, but I get paid for it. And I need to get paid because I have to support myself, having been abandoned by my husband!'

Bruce had the grace to look ashamed.

'I'm sorry, I shouldn't have said that. Look, I'd better be going. Thanks for the lunch.' He got up and almost ran out of the house.

Shocked and miserable, Rowena felt the tears spurting out of her eyes. The doorbell rang, and she picked up a tissue and dabbed helplessly at her face. Let it ring! She wasn't in the mood. Whoever it was could just go away again. But the ringing went on and on, and eventually she got to her feet and went to answer it. Bruce stood on the step, looking sheepish.

'I'm sorry,' he said, brushing past her. 'With all that going on I forgot why I came in the first place. Are my grey trousers still here? I can't seem to find them.'

'Take a look in the wardrobe,' she sniffed. 'I haven't opened the thing since you left. You may as well clear it out while you're at it. Save you coming back another time.'

Hearing her tone, he looked at her in concern.

'What's the matter, Row? I didn't mean to upset you.' He put his arms around her, which made her sob all the harder. The remembered feel of his tweed jacket and the scent of his aftershave were almost too much to bear.

'It wasn't you,' she lied. 'It's something else. Something rather nasty has been happening, and I don't know how to deal with it.'

'A cup of tea, first,' he said briskly, 'and then you can tell me all about it, eh?'

So, while they were sipping scalding hot Darjeeling, she told him about the threatening e-mails.

'And the police weren't interested at all, Bruce. They suggested I change my address, but that's such a nuisance.'

'Do you still have them on the computer?'

'The latest one, yes, I think so. I'll show it to you.'

She booted up the computer and saw that she had mail. She opened it and was startled to see that it was another message from the crank.

Remember what happened to Bettina Nichols. Do you want to go the same way?

Rowena started to shake.

'There, you see? This can't be just a random thing. It's got to be someone who knows me, and, more than that, someone who knows about my aunt's murder.'

'Come and sit down, love.' Bruce led her gently back to the table where she put her head in her hands. 'Let's figure this out. It's almost a quarter of a century since your aunt was killed, and you weren't even living here then. How many people would connect you with that tragedy?'

Rowena shook her head helplessly. It had been a big story at the time, of course, in all the newspapers, but her parents had lived miles away from her father's younger sister. Rowena had only been present at the time of the murder because her aunt was looking after her while they were away having a short break.

Naturally it wasn't something that could ever be forgotten by the family, but in the intervening years Rowena's grandparents had died, and there were few other relatives. Bettina's death had haunted her brother, and the Nichols had eventually gone to Australia to begin a new life.

They had wanted Rowena to go with them, but she had met Bruce, fallen in love and married him, and stayed in England. Her parents, confident that she would be well taken care of by her new husband, had gone abroad with no misgivings.

'I don't know who knows my story,' she said. 'It's not something one usually boasts about. Apart from Mum and Dad, there isn't anyone else.'

She looked at Bruce's face, which

had suddenly turned pink.

'Bruce, no! You haven't told Ariana, have you?'

'Um, yes, I may have done. I mean, you do tell people things, don't you? I didn't see the harm. Anyway,' he went on, 'this has nothing to do with Ariana. She wouldn't do anything like this.'

Oh, wouldn't she? Rowena thought. She made a deliberate play for my husband, and now that things aren't going too well between them she may be feeling insecure. Driving me out of town would be to her advantage, especially if she thinks she can get her hands on this house. No doubt she's tired of living in that grotty little flat over the office.

Bruce scratched the back of his neck, a sure sign that he was feeling uncomfortable.

'Look, love, I can't leave you to deal with this alone. And if the police can't help, perhaps it's time we did a bit of detective work ourselves.'

'I don't know where we'd start. And

what would we be looking for?'

'We'd have a look through the newspaper files in Bettina's town, for a start. Maybe even some of the dailies. I'm sure they would have published a colourful blow-by-blow description of what was said and done at the time. Then we could speak to Bettina's neighbours. There might be someone who remembers seeing something which didn't strike them as unusual at the time, but which took on greater significance after she was killed.'

Rowena shuddered.

'I don't know, Bruce. What if it was one of those neighbours who did it? Say a local man who had designs on Aunt Bettina, but was turned down by her? We could be walking into danger. I think we should let well alone. Maybe it would be best if I did move right away from here. There's nothing to keep me here now,' she added sadly.

'Come on, don't be such a wimp! You'll be safe with me.'

Bruce looked extremely fierce. Despite

her anxiety, Rowena stifled a giggle. Knowing that he was on her side made her feel much better. If they could find some useful evidence, the police might be forced to take her story seriously.

At the time of her death, Aunt Bettina had been living in Minton, a town that was a forty-five-minute drive away.

'I'm free tomorrow and could take a run over there,' Bruce said. 'How about you?'

'Well, yes,' Rowena told him. 'I have a lot of work on hand, but there's no particular deadline. If we don't get back too late I can put in a few hours in the evening.'

Tom had delivered a new batch of boxes the day before so he wasn't likely to turn up, only to find that she wasn't working. In any case, they had agreed that she could choose her own hours.

'So where do we start?'

'At the offices of the local paper, I should think. I'll pick you up as soon as I can get away, say around nine?'

Rowena forbore to ask him if he was going to tell Ariana what he was up to. After all, she and Bruce were still married, officially, so the girl could hardly complain. Or, if she did, Rowena just didn't care!

7

Minton was a fairly large town, and it was some time before they found the offices of the Minton Gazette.

'Why don't we just stop and ask for directions?' Rowena demanded, but Bruce shook his head and continued to drive at a snail's pace, peering out of the window as he went. It was a relief when they finally drew up beside a shabby building on a side street.

'Oh, yes, we have them all on file, downstairs,' the receptionist told them. 'On microfilm, of course. We've only the one machine to view them on, but you're in luck. Nobody else is using it just now, so you can get started immediately if you wish.'

A young reporter guided them down to a cool basement room and showed them the shelves where the boxes of film were stored.

Rowena was pleased to see that the microfilm reader was a modern one, equipped with a coin slot so that copies could be made.

'Well, shall we get on with it?' Bruce was standing beside the shelves, his hand poised to remove a box of film. 'Nineteen seventy-eight, was it?'

'I think so. It must have been June when it happened because Mum and Dad were celebrating their wedding anniversary. They were married on June seventeenth, I believe.'

Bruce turned the handle on the microfilm reader while Rowena sat close to him, peering over his shoulder. The Gazette was a weekly newspaper so there was nothing in the actual week of the murder. It had made front page news the following week.

'Probably scooped by the big dailies,' Bruce muttered. 'If we don't get what we need here, we'll have to go farther afield. Still, this is a start.'

Rowena had lived with the knowledge of her aunt's death for most of her life, but even so, it was a shock to find the story leaping up at her from the page.

Grisly death of local woman. Found strangled in her own home. There was a blurred photo of her aunt, one that she had never seen before.

Had Rowena's father kept all the newspaper accounts of his sister's death? If he had, they had been kept well away from his young daughter. She had a dim memory of coming home from school in tears at about the age of six, after a schoolmate had imparted the information that her aunt had been murdered.

At that age, Rowena didn't even know what the word meant, and looking back, she doubted if the other child had either, but had half understood the story after hearing the grown-ups talking.

Rowena's mother had gently explained that a bad man had hurt Auntie Bettina, who was in heaven now, and had tried to be reassuring when the child tremulously asked if the bad person would come and hurt them, too.

Now it dawned on Rowena for the first time that her parents must have felt just as terrified at the time and in fact, must never have been able to come to terms with what had happened as the intruder had never been caught.

'Look here, Row, there's reams of this stuff. If we start reading it now, we'll be here all day. What say we print out anything that has anything to do with the case, and go through it later?'

After an hour, Bruce had amassed a large pile of photocopies.

'That seems to be about it, by the look of it. My stomach tells me it's time to eat. Shall we go? We can always come back later.'

But Rowena had had enough of the darkened little archive and said she'd like to leave it for another day. So they went to a cheerful little tea room and gorged themselves on homemade Black Forest cake which made her feel much better.

'What next?' Bruce asked. 'I know we've been thinking about interviewing the neighbours, but I feel we'd be better prepared if we read through this stuff first. Then we'd know what questions to ask. Agreed?'

Rowena nodded. They both seemed reluctant to get back in the car and start for home, so without needing to discuss the matter, they found themselves strolling into a nearby park, where they marvelled at the sight of two swans, making their stately way down a tranquil river.

Rowena thought sadly that they had always been on the same wavelength, seeming to know each other's thoughts without putting anything into words, so why was it that they were now living apart?

She felt quite awkward, walking along in close proximity to Bruce. What if anyone they knew happened to see them, and reported this to Ariana? She was being silly, of course. She was the innocent party in all this so why was she being made to feel very much like the other woman?

When their car eventually pulled up in front of Rowena's house, Bruce declined to come in.

'I must go. I promised to take Ariana out dancing tonight.'

Out dancing! The last time he'd taken his wife dancing was on their honeymoon. Even then he'd been reluctant to take to the floor, saying that it just wasn't his thing. Rowena had never tried to persuade him otherwise, but evidently Ariana was made of sterner stuff. She could imagine the girl gyrating in time to the music, tossing back that long hair, while Bruce tried to keep in step, like a lumbering bear.

'So you'd better take this lot,' Bruce said, turning around to retrieve the pile of papers from the back seat. 'I'm sure you'll want to read them without any further delay.'

Rowena began to shiver. The thought of reading all the details of Aunt

Bettina's death was bad enough, without doing that while she herself was alone in the house. Even now the mystery man — or woman — might be getting ready to send out another threat.

'I don't think I can bear to do that when I'm on my own,' she quavered. 'Can't you come back another time and we'll do it together? And I don't think I even want the beastly stuff in the house. Please take it away.'

Bruce seemed to understand.

'Right! I'll lock it away in the office safe for now. I've got a job on first thing in the morning, but I could be here by about eleven. How will that be?'

Rowena nodded gratefully. She watched him drive away, and then went to her computer to catch up on her work.

★   ★   ★

'How was the dancing?'

Bruce groaned.

'I'm aching in every muscle. Whatever happened to nice, old-fashioned waltzes?'

'There are still places where they do ballroom dancing.' Rowena laughed, although she could hardly imagine Ariana in that setting. 'Like a cup of tea before we get down to business?'

'I'd love one. My first today. We're completely out of tea at home. Ariana never seems to have time to go to the supermarket.'

'You'd better pop in on the way back, then,' Rowena told him.

'You never let us run out of things,' he grumbled, looking at her sorrowfully. 'As a matter of fact, I told her that, but she took umbrage at that. Do you know what she told me? Go back to her then, if she's so wonderful!'

Rowena wasn't about to encourage that sort of thing.

'Right! I'll put the kettle on. I thought we'd spread the papers out on the coffee table. I don't want tea cups anywhere near my computer or the files I'm working on.'

The first report told the story much as Rowena knew it. Since she had grown up, her parents had, at her urging, told her a bit more about the tragedy than had first been explained to her. Bettina Nichols had been strangled in her own home in what the police had assumed was a burglary gone wrong.

It was not a case of Miss Nichols having arrived home to find a robbery in progress, the reporter had written, *because there was a young child in the house who would not have been left there alone.*

Miss Nichols was obviously there when the perpetrator arrived and, in fact, must have admitted him — or them — to the house because there was no sign of forced entry. Rowena felt sick when she read that the child was the victim's niece, three-year-old Rowena Nichols, who was a visitor in the home at the time.

Next door neighbours, Valerie and Dominic Bradshaw, were the first to report the crime. 'I thought I heard a thump,' Mrs Bradshaw told our reporter, 'but I didn't think anything of it at first.

I thought Miss Nichols must have knocked over a chair or something. But then the little girl began to cry, and that went on for quite a long time. I thought it was odd that Miss Nichols didn't go up to see to her, but it was none of my business, so I went on with what I was doing for a while.

'But eventually the child's cries got so desperate I thought we'd better go and see what was going on. I said to my hubby, Dom, I said, what if that thump was Miss Nichols falling off a ladder or something, and she's lying there all unconscious? Well, round we went, and found the front door sitting open, and that wasn't right, for a start. Always very particular about security, Miss Nichols was, a young woman living alone. The first thing we saw when we stepped inside was her lying at the foot of the stairs. Just lying there. I came over all of a tremble.'

The article went on to describe poor Bettina, strangled with her own scarf. There had been signs of a struggle

— overturned furniture and smashed crockery.

Bruce looked at Rowena, his face as white as that of the unknown Dominic.

'Rowena, love, this is terrible. I mean, I was well aware of what had happened and I knew that you were there at the time, but this makes it all seem well, real, somehow. It's a miracle that you weren't hurt as well. Do you think the man knew you were there?'

Rowena frowned.

'As I've always said, I can't remember a thing. I was just a toddler. Whose memory goes back that far? Mine certainly doesn't. I must say, though, that reading this stuff gives me the creeps.'

Bruce put his hand over her trembling fingers.

'Yes, well, it's not just that, is it? It's this business of the e-mails. Either somebody is just playing very nasty tricks on you, or they intend to harm you. Either way, they've got to be stopped. Come on, get your coat. We're going back to Minton.'

'What for?'

'Our next step is to interview the Bradshaws. We need a bit more to go on before we go back to the police.'

When they drew up at Number 14, Curlew Lane, where Aunt Bettina had lived in the downstairs flat, Rowena felt extremely apprehensive. But the well-kept brick house didn't seem familiar to her in any way. Nothing struck a chord, whether frightening or otherwise. They rang the bell but there was no response. Neither the downstairs nor the upstairs tenants were at home.

'We'll try next door, then,' Bruce decided. 'Which side did the Bradshaws live on?'

'How should I know? We'll have to try both, I suppose.'

But the woman who opened the door at Number 16 shook her head in surprise.

'Oh, no, dear. They did live at number twelve for many years but they're gone now.'

Rowena scrunched up her face in disappointment.

'Do you mean they've died?'

'Yes and no. Mr Bradshaw, he dropped dead with a heart attack just last year. His widow, now, she's still alive.' A suspicious look came over her face. 'You're not selling something, are you?'

'My wife knew them when she was young,' Bruce put in. 'We were passing through the district and we thought we'd like to look them up. Funny, though, she seemed to recall that they lived at Number 14.'

'Oh, no, dear, that was where the murder took place. Years back, that was, before we moved here, but I've heard the neighbours mention it. In fact, I think it was Val Bradshaw who found the body!'

Bruce chipped in before she could put two and two together.

'Have you any idea where she is now?'

'She went into one of them sheltered housing places in the west end of town.

Sunny Acres, I think it's called.'

Thanking her, they hastened out to the car and drove off.

'Let's hope she doesn't phone up the old girl and tell her we're coming,' Bruce muttered. 'I was rather relying on the element of surprise.'

However, when they arrived at Sunny Acres, it was to find that most of the residents had gone out.

'We have a minibus,' the warden explained. 'Once a week we take them shopping, you see. Of course, they're quite at liberty to shop at other times but that involves crossing the main road to wait for a bus, which is a bit too much for some of the older ladies. Our bus takes them right to the shopping precinct and brings them back after lunch. If you come back around two o'clock, say?'

They had no choice but to agree to that.

'And speaking of lunch . . . ' Bruce said, and they found a quiet pub where they ordered soup and ham rolls.

The door opened and a group of men, dressed in business suits, came in and went up to the bar. One of the men hesitated as he passed their table and Rowena noticed, to her surprise, that it was Tom's uncle. They nodded to each other and he then joined his companions.

'That man seems to know you,' Bruce remarked, breaking his roll in half.

'Yes, his name is Mark Forrest,' Rowena told him. 'He's the uncle of one of the people I work for. We don't really know each other but we have met once or twice in passing.'

On hearing that, Bruce lost interest and they chatted about inconsequential things until it was time to return to Sunny Acres. Mrs Bradshaw was in her sunny little flat and her eyes opened wide with delight when they explained who Rowena was.

'Well, I never did! You're that poor little mite, all grown up. And married, too. This is your husband, I suppose.

How lovely to meet you.'

Bruce allowed her to take him by the hand but ignored the rest of her remark.

'We were in the area,' he said again, 'and we — that is, Rowena here, thought it would be nice to come and look you up.'

'That was thoughtful, dear. I'm only sorry that my Dom isn't here to see you. He would have been so pleased. We often talked about you in the years since it happened, and your poor auntie, too. Wondered how you were getting along, and that.'

Rowena swallowed hard.

'I wondered if you could tell me what really happened that night, with me, I mean. You see, I remember absolutely nothing about it. I was so young when it happened, of course.'

Various emotions showed in the face of the older woman.

'I don't know if I should, dear. Isn't it best to leave all that in the past? It may be a blessing that your mind didn't take it in.'

'No, please, Mrs Bradshaw. It would be easier for me if I knew the truth. Being left in suspense makes one's imagination run riot, you see.'

The old lady nodded slowly.

'Well, if you're sure it's what you want, I'll see what I can do.'

She sat back in her chair, closing her eyes. Then she began the tale she must have told so many times before.

'We knew you were coming to stay for a few days. Poor Miss Nichols said your parents were having an anniversary, their fifth, I think.

'Well, there was this thump and then we heard you start to cry. Our two houses were quite close together, not semi-detached but there was just a narrow passageway in between, not like a proper driveway, you see. Not many people had cars when those places were first built. It was a hot night and we all had our windows open, otherwise we wouldn't have heard anything. As it was, we'd been watching Coronation Street and we'd only just switched the telly off. Had it all happened any earlier the sound wouldn't have carried.'

Rowena nodded, afraid to interrupt in case she stopped the flow.

'Well, the baby — that was you, dear — began to shriek louder and louder. Dom, he looked at me and said how you were working yourself up into a right old tantrum, but it worried me. Miss Nichols didn't seem the sort to ignore a toddler in that condition. You could have fallen out of bed or anything. So I said we'd better go round and that's when we found her. Your aunt.'

'But where was I, Mrs Bradshaw? Please, this is important.'

'That's the funny thing, dear. When I went upstairs, there you were on the landing, the tears rolling down your face like a regular waterfall. The bedroom door was open and I could see a cot, put up beside the poor lady's bed. I suppose she'd got it in special, with you coming to stay. The sides were up, but you must have managed to climb out somehow and I suppose you fell on the floor, and that started you off.'

'Could it have been the thump you heard?' Bruce suggested.

'I doubt it. The child didn't weigh all that much, not at her age, and we'd never have heard that from across the way. No, it's my belief that came about in the struggle, Miss Nichols fighting for her life you might say.'

She put her hand over her mouth.

'There! I promised myself I wouldn't tell any nasty details, and now I've gone and done it. I'm that sorry, Mr Dexter.'

'It's all right, Mrs Bradshaw. We know all about that. We've seen the newspapers,' Bruce assured her. 'And I believe that you took Rowena over to your own home after that.'

'That's right. My Dom, he said we ought to leave everything just as it was until the police came, but I told him not to be so silly. What, leave the poor terrified little soul in a place where there's been a violent death? The police won't have far to come when they want to talk to me, I said.'

Rowena spoke softly to the woman who had rescued her all those years ago.

'That was very kind of you, Mrs Bradshaw. I'm sure my parents were very grateful when they found out about it.'

'They were that. It was a day or two before they knew about it all, them being abroad. The policewoman wanted to take you and put you in a foster home until your people could come, but I wouldn't let you go. You'd just got used to me, so why leave you among strangers when you were so frightened?'

'Oh, I expect I soon got over it,' Rowena said. 'I wouldn't be the first child to fall out of her cot. I probably wasn't hurt much at all.'

Mrs Bradshaw turned to face Rowena, her eyes wide.

'Oh, but that wasn't it, dear. Oh, no, it was the man.'

'What man?' Rowena felt a strange sensation, as though icy fingers had wandered up her spine.

'You kept saying, 'Nasty man! Make the nasty man go away.' Over and over you said it.'

'I don't recall seeing a mention of this in the papers,' Bruce said. 'Of course, we've only seen the local paper. Maybe there was more in the big dailies or nationals, even.'

Mrs Bradshaw shook her head.

'I never told anyone about it, not even the police. Dom, he kept on at me to report it, but I wouldn't do it. She's had an upset, I said, why make matters worse? It's not as if telling them would help them find the murderer. She's far too young to give a description of any kind. And maybe it would be safer if nobody did know. The murderer might not know anything about kiddies, and wouldn't understand about a toddler being too young to say what she saw. You could have been in danger as well, if that got out, Rowena.'

As I still am, Rowena thought, her stomach churning.

Both Bruce and Rowena were quiet on the way back from Minton. By the intent look on Bruce's face as he drove, she knew that many conflicting thoughts were going through his mind. It wasn't until they drew up in front of her house that he had his say.

'Rowena, love, I'm more convinced than ever now that those e-mails are connected with your aunt's death.'

'So am I, but who is it? And why now, after twenty-five years? It makes no sense at all.'

'I agree, and that's why we can't go back to the police just yet. You've reported the earlier calls, which they dismissed as the work of somebody who thinks it's funny to go round frightening people, as it may well be. Now we've learned from Mrs Bradshaw that you witnessed the crime, or at least saw a man in your aunt's house at the time of her death, but if you tell that bit to the police, it won't get them any further ahead, will it?'

'And meanwhile I could be in danger,' Rowena cried.

Without warning, tears spurted from her eyes, and the next moment she found herself in her husband's arms, sobbing as if her heart would break.

All the pent-up emotions of the past few weeks came rushing out. If asked to explain herself at that moment she would have been unable to say whether it was the stress of the visit to Mrs Bradshaw that was affecting her so badly, or the shock and grief at Bruce's defection. Possibly some of both.

Bruce gently led her into the house and put the kettle on, automatically going to the places where the cups, tea and sugar were kept, as he had so often done in the past.

'I'm so scared, Bruce! I don't think I can stay here alone tonight. I just can't.'

'You don't have to, love,' he said soothingly. 'I'll stay with you, in the spare room,' he added, as her head came up and she looked at him with dawning hope. 'I'll have to ring up Ariana and tell her I won't be home until the morning.'

The thought that home now meant the flat where he lived with Ariana hit Rowena in the pit of her stomach, but she was grateful for small mercies. She tried not to listen as Bruce explained himself to his girlfriend, and by the audible squawking that came from the other end of the line, that did not go well. Of course, his excuses didn't sound plausible because he had to keep quiet about what was behind Rowena's need to have him stay.

Rowena wondered if the e-mail messages would now come thick and fast, if indeed Ariana was behind them. In a way, that might be a good thing. She could believe that Ariana might do her best to frighten off her rival, but not that the girl would use physical violence against her.

Better to have a jealous girlfriend to deal with than the other alternative, that the murderer was now, for some weird reason, on her trail. And as he had never been caught, he was probably still out there somewhere . . .

That night, despite her worries, Rowena had a better night's sleep than she had done since starting to live alone. The knowledge that Bruce was nearby, only separated from her by an inside wall, was tremendously comforting. It was also wonderful to have him sitting beside her at the breakfast table the next morning, using his toast to mop up the residue of the eggs she had poached in just the way he liked them.

'Will you be all right now, love?' Bruce looked at her with concern as he stood up, retrieving his jacket from the back of his chair.

'I feel much better now,' she said truthfully. 'And I've plenty of work to keep me busy so I won't have as much time to think.'

'Look, I have a contract to deal with that will take me out of town for three days, but I'll check in on you after that,

OK? Maybe we can do a bit more sleuthing, look up the daily newspapers and see if they reported anything The Gazette missed.'

'You sound like Miss Marple,' Rowena told him, and he grinned.

8

Rowena jumped when the phone rang, and she had to force herself to pick it up. She let out a sigh of relief when the familiar voice of the author, Morgan Evans, boomed at her.

'I've a manuscript for you to put on discus,' he told her.

'Disk,' she corrected automatically. 'That was fast. I thought you'd only just started working on your new book.'

'What? Oh, no, this isn't my new work. It's something I wrote years ago, when I was just starting out. It was rejected then, as manuscripts by unknown writers often are, but I've kept it by me, and now my publishers are interested in bringing it out. They think it will sell now that I'm a name as you might say. I've looked it over and I must say it's not bad. Not bad at all. I've made quite a few changes, tightened it up here and there, and I think it will do.'

Rowena agreed to go to his cottage and pick it up. She did wonder what was stopping him from delivering it to her, but she didn't really mind as it would get her out of the house. In any case she wanted to stop in at the office with the latest batch of work so she might as well make a morning of it.

Pauline greeted her with a red nose and streaming eyes.

'I think I'm allergic to all these paint fumes,' she grumbled, mopping at herself with a sodden tissue. 'Don't you agree they should send me home sick? I don't suppose you'd like to take over from me for a few days, would you?'

'You forget, I'm already temping here.' Rowena laughed. 'I may not be here every day, but I do keep my nose to the grindstone at home.'

'Then how about letting me move in with you? They could re-route the office calls there! Only joking,' she added hastily, seeing Rowena's hesitation.

Rowena had almost finished transferring her work on to the main office computer, when Tom Forrest rushed in.

'What a morning!' he groaned.

'Did it go badly in court?'

'You could say that. A curse on all clients who hire a barrister to defend them, and then speak out of turn! Never mind, it's over now. Are you free for lunch?'

Pleased, Rowena said that she was. They walked to the same little restaurant where they'd eaten together on previous occasions, and as they sat down to consult the menu she felt the tensions of the previous day ebbing away. They had reached the dessert stage when Tom took a deep breath and said, 'There's something I need to know, Rowena.'

'Oh, yes?'

'I'll come straight to the point. Uncle Mark mentioned that he'd come across you having lunch in a pub yesterday, with a man.'

Rowena was taken aback. Why on

earth would this be of interest to Tom, or to Mark Forrest, for that matter?

'Well, yes, I do remember seeing him there, as a matter of fact.'

'And the man you were with, is he someone special?'

Biting down a scathing retort, she made herself answer quietly.

'He was at one time, Tom. I was having lunch with Bruce, my estranged husband.'

He relaxed visibly.

'Oh, I see. And of course, with the divorce coming up, you have a lot to discuss.'

Rowena couldn't imagine where all this was leading, and she certainly didn't have to explain herself to this man, who after all was just her employer, but she had nothing to hide, did she?

'Actually, we haven't done anything about filling for divorce yet. We did decide how to divide our assets, of course, but that happened more or less naturally. Bruce moved out of the house when he went to Ariana. I was already there and saw no reason to move. Bruce kept the accountancy firm for the simple reason that he is the firm. I'm not an accountant, as you know, so without Bruce there is nothing.'

Tom nodded sympathetically.

'But you will be divorcing in due course?'

'I suppose so. There just doesn't seem to be any need to rush into it at present. Not unless one of us wants to re-marry. Bruce hasn't said anything about his plans with Ariana, and I certainly have nothing in mind.'

'Unless you fall in love again,' he said softly, 'with someone who really appreciates you.'

'That's not very likely, is it?'

Rowena studied her plate, remembering the pain of rejection when Bruce had come home and announced that he was leaving her for the gorgeous younger woman.

Tom took her hand.

'Look at me, Rowena. As I've said

before, your husband must have been mad to leave you. You're beautiful, intelligent and kind. What more could any man want?'

Embarrassed, she made no reply.

'The thing is, Rowena, I think I'm falling in love with you.'

Oh, dear. Now what was she supposed to say? She wanted to come up with a witty answer, but what came out was a silly, 'Are you?' which she wished she could bite back as soon as she had said it. Luckily, Tom didn't appear to notice her confusion.

'Yes, I am. I didn't mean to pry into your private life, but when Uncle Mark mentioned that you were seeing some-one, I had to know if I'm wasting my time. There isn't anyone else, is there, Rowena?'

'No, there isn't,' she murmured.

'Well, then, could we start going out on an official basis?'

'I'd like that, Tom, but I'm afraid I can't promise anything more than friendship. I do like you, in fact, I like you very much, but I'm just not ready to take anything to the next level, whatever that may be.'

He nodded.

'I appreciate your candour. I understand that you've only been separated for a short time, and of course that didn't happen by your own wish. You must feel betrayed and confused, and unwilling to commit to anybody new. Let's leave it at that, then. We'll go out together from time to time and if that leads to something more, so be it.'

Rowena wished that she could talk to Jude about this. She was touched by Tom's apparent sensitivity and wanted to tell somebody that her faith in men had been restored by what he had said.

As she walked home she let her thoughts drift to a possible future with Tom. He was bright, hard working and successful. If she married him she would want for nothing, and some day — in the far future, she hoped, because of course she didn't wish any harm to his parents — he would inherit

Courtneys and they would spend their lives in those beautiful surroundings.

It would be such a wonderful place in which to bring up children. Tom would want children, of course, to inherit the family home in their turn. He had spoken of his young days there, of taking part in pony club events, and having tennis parties as a teenager. Naturally he would want his own youngsters to enjoy all the things which went with such a privileged lifestyle.

Given time, could she possibly fall in love with him? There was no way that she could bring herself to marry a man simply for his wealth and position. Love might come in time, but first she had to erase Bruce from her heart and mind, and she didn't know if she would ever be able to do that.

★ ★ ★

Bruce phoned. Rowena could tell by his hushed tones that he didn't want Ariana to overhear what he was saying.

'I've got a few slack days ahead. I thought we might go and investigate the daily newspapers we spoke of.'

'Oh, dear!' Rowena was in a dilemma. She very much wanted to go with him, but she was suddenly swamped with work.

'It's Morgan Evans,' she explained. 'I told you about having to type an old manuscript of his, didn't I? I've really got to concentrate on this one or I'll make terrible errors.'

Instead of re-typing his early work, the author had covered the old manuscript with scribbled sentences and yellow stickers. He had also added several new pages without proper directions as to where the material should be inserted. She had thought of suggesting that he should re-do the whole thing before she started work, but was afraid that he would huffily refuse, asking her what she thought he was paying her for. That being the case, the only way she could keep the plot straight in her head was to keep going, with as few breaks as possible.

Fortunately, Bruce understood.

'That's OK. I'll do it myself and make copies of anything interesting, as we did before. This doesn't really need two of us. You get on with your job, and I'll get back to you when I have something to report.'

Later, Rowena jumped when the phone rang. Busily engaged in a particularly tricky part of Morgan Evans' manuscript, she was half inclined not to answer. It couldn't be anyone she wanted to hear from, anyway. Mum wouldn't be calling from Australia in what, for them, would be the early hours of the morning; Bruce was out of town, and Tom usually contacted her by e-mail. Neither would it be Miss Benson, who knew that Rowena already had more work than she could comfortably handle.

But the rings kept coming, and with a sigh of exasperation Rowena snatched up the receiver with a curt hello.

A quavery voice answered.

'Is this Mrs Dexter? Mrs Rowena Dexter?'

'Yes, that's right. Can I help you?' Rowena calmed down on realising that the caller was an elderly woman.

'Oh, thank goodness! I've tried so hard to get in touch with you. I did contact the office of a Mr Bruce Dexter, an accountant, thinking that was your husband, but a very rude young woman told me that you weren't there, and that you had no connection with him at all.'

Ariana, of course. Before Rowena could formulate a diplomatic answer, the woman was going on with her tale.

'So I've tried all the Dexters in the phone book, and you won't believe how many there are!'

'Um, who are you, please?' This was getting them nowhere, and Rowena was eager to get back to her work.

'Oh, didn't I say? This is Val Bradshaw, dear. Remember, you came to see me the other day, you and your husband?'

'That's right. Have you thought of something else to tell me?'

'Not exactly, but I had to let you know, dear. I may have done something a bit silly.'

'I'm not sure I follow,' Rowena replied, puzzled.

'Well, dear, there's been a man, wanting to know about the old days when we lived next door to your poor auntie. Just imagine, it's been left back in the past all these years, and now suddenly I've had two lots of visitors inside a week, wanting to talk about it.'

'What sort of man, Mrs Bradshaw? A newspaper reporter, perhaps?'

'I don't think so. Quite distinguished looking, really, like you imagine a college professor would be. He told me he was gathering research for a book of local history, and he wanted to know about the murder. He seemed very nice, and I was feeling a bit lonely that day, it being the anniversary of my Dom's death, so I'm afraid I let my tongue run away with me a bit. I said if he wanted to know more he should get in touch with you.'

Her voice faltered.

'I told him about you keeping on about the bad man you saw. He was quite interested in that. I thought afterwards that I shouldn't have let him know about it, not after keeping quiet all these years. And that's why I'm phoning. They've never caught the killer, have they, so what if that writer puts what I said in the book and . . . ' Her voice petered out.

Rowena tried to pass it off lightly.

'Thank you for letting me know, Mrs Bradshaw, but the book might not even get published, and even if it does, there's no guarantee that the killer will read it. He probably went as far away as possible after it all happened, abroad, even.'

After twittering on for several more minutes, Mrs Bradshaw rang off, comforted. Not so Rowena. Evidently she and Bruce were not the only ones investigating Bettina's murder, and wasn't it too much of a coincidence that someone was looking into the story at the same time? She had a horrid feeling that the man who had killed Aunt Bettina was not very far away at all, and in fact might be coming nearer. She wished desperately that Bruce would hurry back.

When he did return he had little to show for his efforts and was inclined to disparage what he had achieved.

'The big dailies had plenty to say for a while, although I must say that the local paper seems to have covered the story pretty well. I did make copies of everything I found but a second reading has shown me that I haven't turned up much. When the police failed to make an arrest the journalists seem to have lost interest, or rather other stories broke and they followed those instead.'

'Weren't there any suspects?'

'Not really. I've heard that when a woman dies under suspicious circumstances the police investigate the husband first. Your aunt wasn't married, of course, so they zeroed in on the boyfriend, one Mark Collins. He had an unbreakable alibi, though, having been at some family reunion at the time of the murder, where he was seen by umpteen people. Oh, and your friend, Val Bradshaw, was to the forefront once again.'

Bruce skimmed through his pile of clippings.

'Here we are. *Asked whether she had noticed any visitors or strangers near Bettina Nichols' flat on the fateful evening, next-door neighbour, Valerie Bradshaw, stated that she could not have done.*

'*We were busy watching Coronation Street, same as usual. I never went outside until we went round to see what was wrong with the kiddie. That was when we found the body.*'

'That reminds me,' Rowena put in. 'I had a call from Mrs Bradshaw while you were gone. Apparently she had tried to get in touch with you but got the brush off from Ariana. She was upset enough to keep trying all the Dexters in the book until she located me. Although why it didn't occur to her that R. Dexter might be me, I don't know. That's how most single women list themselves, using an initial rather than a name.'

Bruce frowned.

'Funny that. Ariana didn't say anything about a call from Mrs Bradshaw.'

I bet she didn't, Rowena thought, but she didn't say it aloud.

'Of course, now I come to think of it, when we went to see her that day we did nothing to suggest to her the notion that we are still man and wife.'

'Never mind that. What did she want?'

Rowena repeated what Mrs Bradshaw had told her, and he frowned again.

'I don't like the sound of that. Do you suppose it was the gentleman friend, Mark Collins, coming out of the woodwork?'

Now it was Rowena's turn to frown.

'According to the newspaper reports the boyfriend was ruled out as a suspect. And this one here says the official verdict was murder by a person or persons unknown which is what they usually say when they haven't a clue. In fact, we're right back to what was suggested by the local paper, that Aunt Bettina was probably killed during a burglary that went wrong.'

'So now, a quarter century later, we've got a middle-aged thug going round pretending to be researching a local history book?' Bruce's tone was scornful. 'In that case, why didn't he bump off Mrs Bradshaw as well?'

They were going round in circles and getting nowhere. By this time Rowena was close to tears and she didn't care if Bruce saw it.

'I'm exhausted,' he muttered. 'I think we'd better call it a day.'

He pushed the newspaper copies to the edge of the table and left the house, saying that he'd be in touch.

Rowena had a welcome break from work and worry when Tom invited her out to Courtneys at the weekend. His eldest niece, a child called Prudence, was riding in her first pony club gymkhana, and her proud parents wanted the whole family to be there to encourage her. After calling at the house to collect Tom's parents, the four of them drove off to a neighbouring estate, where the event was being held.

There were horse boxes all over the place, and they could hear announcements blaring over a public address system. Youngsters in jodhpurs and hard hats were busily saddling up their ponies and half listening to last minute instructions from officious parents.

Mr and Mrs Forrest were smiling in anticipation of a pleasant time, watching their granddaughter in action. Leaving the car with the other parked vehicles, the four of them crossed a muddy field to the ringside, where Tom's sister, Deborah, greeted them with enthusiasm.

'How's Prue?' her fond grandmother asked. 'Not too nervous, I hope?'

'Oh, no, she's lapping it all up like a veteran. As a matter of fact, you've got here just in time. They'll be calling her class in a minute.'

Rowena watched with interest as several small children, mounted on equally small ponies, and with numbers attached to their jackets, took their places in the ring. Rowena was happy to see that Prue was quite efficient at getting her pony to walk and trot at the judge's commands, and she clapped wildly along with the Forrests when the child emerged with a third place rosette.

'A good start,' Tom's father beamed. 'She'll soon have a wall full of the things, just like you did when you were a child, Debs.'

After the more formal classes the day was far from over. They had to wait until Prue took part in a mounted version of musical chairs, in which she finished last, and then a potato and spoon race in which she joyfully claimed second prize.

By lunch time they were ready to go back to Courtneys for a reviving drink and a meal. Deborah wanted to load her daughter's pony into the horsebox and head off with them, but Prue would have none of it.

'I want to stay and see the rest, Mummy,' she protested.

'Oh, we might as well, I suppose,' Deborah said. 'It's the older riders to come now. I should let her watch. She may pick up some tips from the more experienced ones. You lot go on ahead. We'll see you later.'

So Rowena went back to the house with Tom and his parents and enjoyed a relaxed lunch. Mr Forrest mixed up a batch of mimosas, a drink that was new to Rowena.

'Champagne and orange juice,' he beamed. 'We have to celebrate young Prue's first wins, eh?'

A variety of breads, sandwich fillings and fruit were put out on the sideboard by Mrs Forrest, and they were told to help themselves. Tom made a giant sandwich of roast beef liberally smeared with Dijon mustard while Rowena fixed up a more ladylike snack of smoked salmon on wholewheat bread. She was beginning to feel slightly dizzy after all the toasts, and was anxious to soak up the champagne with food before she made a fool of herself.

Tom's father was a marvellous host, and put her at ease immediately by asking about her taste in music and art. Here she was on firm ground, and on hearing that she enjoyed classical jazz, he bore her off to his study to listen to his vast collection of tapes, which she envied greatly. The rest of the day flew by and when it was time to leave she was told that she must not leave it too long before she came again.

She had the feeling that Tom was quite pleased with the way things had gone, as if it was important to him that his parents had taken a liking to her.

It did seem as if they were becoming quite at ease in each other's company. If their love was meant to be, then they would slip into it gradually, which might not be a bad thing, after what had happened to her before.

9

Intent on her work, Rowena was annoyed when the doorbell rang. Why was she getting so many interruptions these days? Bruce had called earlier to say that he meant to come over when he had completed something he was working on, but that wasn't until after lunch, so it couldn't be him now.

She was very surprised to find Tom's uncle waiting at the door, and she invited him in with her heart thumping. Why on earth was he here? If he wanted to speak to her, what was wrong with the telephone?

'Is everything all right?' she stammered. 'Has anything happened to Tom?'

'Tom is quite well, as far as I know.'

The older man stared at her so intently that she felt uncomfortable. She said nothing, waiting for him to continue. All she could think of was that he had come to warn her off. Perhaps he — or the rest of the Forrests — were aware of her growing closeness to Tom and felt that she wouldn't make a suitable bride for the heir to Courtneys. She was, after all, a married woman, soon to be divorced, and although there was no stigma attached to divorce and remarriage nowadays, the Forrests knew nothing of her background.

Tom knew that she was the innocent party, namely, that Bruce had left her for somebody else, but that didn't necessarily mean that he had told his parents that, or if he had, that they believed her side of the story.

'You've been seeing a lot of my nephew, haven't you?' Mark said.

'And you've come to tell me to go away, is that it?'

Rowena tilted her chin aggressively, refusing to be intimidated by him, although her legs were shaking underneath her long denim skirt.

'Oh, it's far too late for that, my dear. If only you'd paid attention to my e-mail messages things might have been different, but it's now come to the point where I must take other steps to resolve the situation.'

Rowena's jaw dropped.

'You sent me those messages! But why? I hardly knew Tom when they started coming. He's had his pick of girlfriends. What made you think he'd choose me, or do you send threats to everyone he goes out with?'

He smiled. She noticed for the first time that he had a wolfish expression, except that wolves didn't have those curious eyes.

'Wait a minute! How did you get my e-mail address in the first place? And how did you know about Aunt Bettina? What happened to her is something I've worked hard at to forget, and I've certainly never said anything to Tom along those lines. And my name is Dexter now, so how could anyone connect me with her?'

He smiled again, but his eyes were cold.

'Getting your address was simple enough. All I had to do was look up your personal file. All your details are there, including your maiden name of Nichols. I'm at chambers quite often, you know. I do work for the firm from time to time. And as for your connection with Bettina, why, my dear, all you have to do is look in the mirror. It gave me quite a turn, I assure you, when I met you at the office that day. It quite took me back, I must say.'

The penny still hadn't dropped.

'You knew my aunt, Mr Forrest?'

'Oh, yes, I knew your aunt, my dear. And my name is not Forrest, it's Collins.'

All at once, everything fell into place. Rowena felt sick. This, then, was Aunt Bettina's former boyfriend, the man who had been taken in to assist the police in their enquiries and later released. Now she was in the same room with him, and, putting two and two together at last, she knew that this man was her aunt's killer!

Her thoughts in a whirl, she knew that she had to keep him talking, no matter how silly the conversation. She had no idea how she was going to get away from him, but the longer she could delay the inevitable, the better. Would she be able to think of something to save herself?

'Collins?' she gasped. 'Not Forrest? But aren't you Tom's uncle?'

'Certainly I am. I'm his mother's brother. John Forrest doesn't have any brothers. I should have thought you'd have found that out by now.'

Rowena took a deep breath.

'So it was you who killed my aunt?'

'Got it in one, my dear.'

'But why? What did she ever do to you?'

'Played me false, Mrs Dexter. She was a charming little thing, you know, a laughing girl. Full of life and high spirits. I was going to ask her to marry me, you see. We'd have made a great partnership.

'We were supposed to be going out together that evening. I'd booked a table at an elegant restaurant, the sort of place with soft music and candlelight. I'd even hired a musician to come to our table to play our song on the violin. I had a red rose to give her. What girl could resist a proposal under those circumstances?'

His eyes looked far away, remembering.

'So what happened?'

Rowena quailed when he swung round to face her, his eyes blazing.

'What happened is that when I went to pick her up as we had arranged, she told me she'd forgotten all about it. Her brother and his wife were away for the weekend, celebrating their wedding anniversary, and she was looking after their child. Naturally I was very put out and told her so, but she only laughed.

'She said that in all the excitement of the child coming our date had slipped her mind. I can still see her shrugging when she told me that it didn't matter, did it? We could go out another time.

'Couldn't she ask the woman next door to come to sit with the child, I asked, but she refused. She said she'd only just got you down to sleep. You were already unsettled by being in a strange place without your parents and she wouldn't dream of leaving you with someone you didn't know. I tried again. I explained how I'd made very special plans for a romantic evening, during which I was meaning to ask her to marry me.

'Do you know what she said? 'Oh, Mark, don't be so silly, we wouldn't suit each other at all.' And she laughed again. Just like that, she laughed in my face.'

'That must have been very painful for you,' Rowena murmured, but if she thought that sympathy was going to get her out of a dangerous situation, she was very much mistaken.

'It was all your fault!' he shouted. 'If it hadn't been for you, everything would have gone as planned. All my perfect arrangements, spoiled by a little brat!'

Rowena knew then that he was truly out of his mind. Had he shown symptoms of an unbalanced personality twenty-five years earlier? Was that why Bettina had rejected him, trying to pass it off as a joke to let him down lightly, because she feared he might go off the deep end?

'So you killed her.' Rowena realised that her hands were clenched so tightly that her fingernails had cut into her palms.

'I didn't mean to kill her, not at first. I took her by the shoulders and shook her. All I wanted to do was make her see reason, but she pulled away from me and ran out of the room, knocking over a small table as she went. I caught up with her and, yes, I throttled her. She didn't take long to die, Rowena. She didn't suffer long.'

'And then you ran off and left her lying there,' Rowena said scornfully.

'Well, of course I did. When I came

to my senses and understood what I'd done it hit me that my career, and my whole life in fact, were in jeopardy unless I could get away. I was pretty sure that nobody saw me arrive, and there was nobody about when I left. I'd had to leave my car round the corner because there wasn't room to park in front of Bettina's place. Those houses didn't have their own garages, or even proper driveways, so anyone that owned a car had to park in the street.'

'But weren't you afraid that you might have left fingerprints at the flat? Didn't the police test you for that?'

'Huh! I was quite often at the flat, so naturally my prints would be all over the place. My being there so much gave me another advantage. The police asked me if I thought anything had been taken, and I described a few bits of jewellery and a silver cup. Your father was asked to corroborate this, but he wasn't in any position to say what Bettina owned. It was years since he and his sister had lived in the same house, and who was to say what bits and pieces she might have accumulated since then? I also said that she was in the habit of keeping money in a kitchen drawer, and that was gone, too.'

'And did she? Keep money in a drawer, I mean?'

He shrugged.

'How should I know? It's the sort of thing people do. That's why they get themselves robbed.'

Rowena was overwhelmed by all this mass of detail.

If this were a television movie, she thought, I'd be wearing some sort of recording device. I'd have this confession on tape.

But as things stood she was the only person alive who knew his story, and she knew herself to be in deadly danger. He would have to kill her now. His terrible secret would go with her to the grave.

'I think I can understand why you killed my aunt,' she told him, trying to keep her voice steady. 'You feel she treated you badly, but why did you stalk me, after all these years? I've never done anything to you.'

'You were there,' he said simply. 'I looked up and saw you standing at the top of the stairs. I didn't know how much you might have seen, especially when you started to bawl. I was on tenterhooks for weeks afterwards, in case you might have said something to help the police to trace me. When nothing happened it seemed I'd got away with it.

'I assumed that a three-year-old child, as I later learned that you were, didn't have the vocabulary to explain what she had seen, but when we met again this year I was afraid that seeing me might have triggered some memory. Then, when I went to see Val Bradshaw — such a gullible woman. She let slip that you had spoken to her about seeing a man that evening.'

'She told me that, too,' Rowena said, 'but actually I have had absolutely no memory of that night at all. My parents believe that I must have been so frightened that I blotted it out, but surely one doesn't retain memories from the toddler years? I was so young then, you know. I'd just had my third birthday.'

'In that case this is really unfortunate, but it's too late to change things now,' Mark Collins murmured, taking a step towards her.

She screamed and ran from the room. History repeating itself, she thought wildly. He was behind her in an instant, grabbing her by the shoulder. Desperately twisting around she managed to bring up her knee to hit him. He gave a roar of pain and rage but he still staggered towards her, catching her as she attempted to flee up the stairs.

He turned at the sound of a key in the lock.

'Are you there, Rowena? I finished work early so I thought I might as well come on over and take you to lunch.'

Bruce stopped in amazement at the tableau that met his eyes. He was knocked sideways as Collins charged by him into the street. Rowena collapsed on to the bottom stairs and began to cry, the tears wrenched out of her painfully.

'What on earth was that?' Bruce gathered her into his arms and held her close, attempting to soothe her.

'Call the police! Call the police!' she squeaked, when at last she could get the words out. 'It's the man who killed Aunt Bettina. Don't let him get away!'

Bruce hesitated, still not quite sure what had happened, but seeing that Rowena was close to hysteria he picked up the phone and dialled. Having managed to convince the police that a crime had been committed, or at least narrowly averted, he then called their doctor, despite her protests that she would be all right.

Then, having settled her in an armchair with a blanket and a hot water bottle, he demanded to be told what had been happening. He listened in growing horror as she stumbled through her story, wide-eyed with remembered fear.

'But what on earth made you let him in, Rowena? How could you be so stupid? What do you have a peephole in the door for? You should have called the police at once.'

Her lower lip trembled.

'I didn't know he was Mark Collins, did I? He's Tom Forrest's uncle. He even looks a bit like him. I thought his name was Forrest, too. How was I supposed to make the connection? Mark is a common enough name.'

'I wish I'd been here earlier. He wouldn't have tried anything with me in the house.'

Rowena shuddered.

'He came here with the express purpose of killing me, Bruce. I'm sure he'd have made some excuse for having called round, and then he would have come back another time. It's not as if you live here at the house, is it?'

She spoke bitterly. Just six months ago she had been happily married to Bruce, working with him in the business they owned together. It was only because he had left her that she had been forced to seek out other work, which in turn had led to her meeting with Mark Forrest, or Collins, as she must think of him now.

★ ★ ★

The doctor arrived at the same time as two police officers. One was a kindly, middle-aged policewoman, the other whom Rowena recognised as the man she had reported the e-mail threats to. The recognition was mutual, she could tell that by the resigned look in his eyes. He obviously had her pegged as an attention-seeking sort of woman, always making mountains out of molehills.

While the policewoman was allowed to be present while the doctor examined Rowena, the sitting-room door was closed firmly on Bruce and her male colleague.

'Now, sir, what's this all about? The young lady's had another fright, has she?'

'A fright! I should say she has! If I hadn't arrived when I did, there would have been another tragedy. He was about to strangle her!'

'What makes you think that, sir?'

The constable still had to be convinced. Bruce groaned.

'Look, I know this was before your time, and it happened over at Minton, but my wife's aunt was murdered twenty-five years ago. My wife, who was then a toddler, may have witnessed the attack. She was certainly present in the house at the time. This man, Mark Collins, was under suspicion then, but cleared of any involvement because he had a cast-iron alibi.'

'So for some reason he came here today to try to frighten Mrs Dexter? I mean, doesn't it sound unlikely to you?'

'I've told you!' Bruce roared, thoroughly out of patience now. 'He came here and confessed to the whole sorry business of Bettina Nichols' death, and then he meant to kill Rowena to stop her coming to you with the story. Much good it would have done her if she had,' he added. 'You don't seem to want to accept anything you're told.'

'All right, sir, we'll look into it, of course. As soon as Mrs Dexter has calmed down we'll take a statement, and follow on from there.'

'Look, I know all this sounds far-fetched, but can't you at least set the wheels in motion to stop this man before he tries to leave the country, or something?'

Still not totally convinced, but seeing the sense of what Bruce had to say, the constable pulled out his mobile phone and began to issue orders.

The living-room door opened and the doctor emerged.

'I've given her a sedative,' he announced. 'I suggest you get her to bed at once. You can ask her questions in the morning, not before. She's had a severe shock, and must have time to recover.' He bustled off, apparently not at all interested in the drama that was unfolding around him.

'Don't leave me,' Rowena wailed, as the police officers prepared to leave. 'I don't want to be on my own. He might come back and try again. Please, please don't leave me!'

Rather awkwardly, Bruce explained that he and Rowena were separated, and he was unable to stay.

'I'm afraid my partner is expecting me home for dinner, and we're going on to a party later. I'll be for the high jump if I'm late.'

The policewoman gave him an old-fashioned look. She made it plain that, separated or not, she didn't have much time for a man who could walk away from Rowena at such a moment. After a hurried consultation with her fellow officer she agreed to stay the night.

'Come on, love, I'll help you upstairs, and you can show me where you sleep. Is there somewhere that I can kip down tonight? And don't fret if you hear someone at the door. I'll have to send for my nightclothes and all that, and I hope you won't mind if I bring in a take-out meal. You won't want me leaving to go to a restaurant, will you?'

Still shaking, Rowena agreed that she would not.

* * *

The next day, with the kindly policewoman still in attendance, a member of the detective squad questioned Rowena.

'I'd like to get your story today, Mrs Dexter, if you feel up to it, and when you feel better I'll ask you report to the station to sign your statement, which we'll get typed up in the meantime. Now, if you're quite ready, we'll start from the beginning, shall we?'

Haltingly, Rowena began to tell him about her aunt's death, but he stopped her there.

'No need to go into that at the moment, Mrs Dexter. We've retrieved all the case notes from the files and we know what happened then. What you know about the crime is only hearsay, of course. I understand from your husband that you have no memory of the events of that time, having been so young.'

Rowena nodded. He smiled at her reassuringly, an older man with greying red hair and twinkling brown eyes.

'So let's start with the threatening messages, shall we? Can we have a look at those?'

Rowena booted up the computer and indicated the messages she had saved. She half expected to see another one sent from Mark Collins, but nothing appeared. At the detective's request she printed them out and handed them to him.

'Of course, this wasn't the start of it all, although I didn't know it at the time. I work as a temp and the agency sent me to the law firm where Mark Collins' nephew is a partner. I ran into him there, quite by accident, and apparently he got an awful shock because I look a lot like Auntie did, when he knew her.'

'So when you were told that nothing could be done about the messages, you decided to do some sleuthing on your own. Never a good idea, Mrs Dexter. I do wish that members of the public would leave these things to us.'

Rowena shot him an indignant look. However, she went on to explain what she and Bruce had done, not achieving a lot of anything, as it happened.

The detective nodded.

'That fills in the background quite nicely, I think. Now, what we need is a complete description of what was said when Collins was here in your home. I want you to be very careful with this. If we are to make the charges stick we must know exactly what happened. Please don't try to say what you felt at the time, or what you only feared he intended to do. Plain, unvarnished facts, please.'

Rowena took a deep breath, and launched into her story. She hesitated from time to time, swallowing hard, but the motherly policewoman took her by the hand and gave it a comforting squeeze.

The detective took careful notes in addition to taping Rowena's story. Occasionally he asked her to go over some point a second time, coming at it from another angle. By the time it was all over she felt quite weak, but it was a relief to get it all off her mind.

She jumped when the detective's mobile phone shrilled. After some terse questions he put it back in the case he wore at his belt, and smiled kindly at her.

'You'll be glad to know that Collins has been apprehended, Mrs Dexter. He was stopped at Heathrow, just before boarding a plane for Canada. In view of what he tried to do here, the judge has refused bail, so you can rest easy tonight.'

'Thank goodness for that,' Rowena breathed. 'Will he be tried for killing Aunt Bettina, or did that happen too long ago?'

'The case will be re-opened and

should come to trial eventually. The only thing is, you'll be required to testify in court when the time comes. We wouldn't have much of a case without you.'

She nodded.

'I'll do whatever it takes to get him put behind bars. I wonder what the jury will make of it all, though? What it comes down to is my word against his.'

'Never mind that. He's made things worse for himself by coming out of the woodwork now. If, as he says, he killed your aunt in a moment of rage, then that might have been taken into consideration if he had turned himself in at the time. Covering his tracks all these years, and then making plans to kill you in cold blood has put a completely different complexion on it.'

'Who gave him the alibi?' Rowena wondered. 'Some other girlfriend, perhaps?'

'Classified information, Mrs Dexter. It will all come out in due course.'

★　★　★

After they had gone Rowena sank back on the settee and thought things over. Did the Forrests know that Mark Collins had been arrested? For the first time in her life she understood that the families of murderers and other criminals probably suffered almost as much as their innocent victims. What would Tom be feeling now? She longed to give him a call, but decided it would be better not to. If he chose to contact her, he knew where she lived.

As she had feared, journalists came from far and wide in search of the story. Bruce suggested she call a Press conference.

'Get it all over at one time. If you don't, they'll never go away. You don't have to face them on your own, Rowena. I'll come and be there with you when you speak to them.'

'The police told me I'm not supposed to give details of his confession before the trial.'

'Of course not, but you can give them a few crumbs to satisfy them. You know, human interest stuff. 'I was the baby on the landing', that sort of thing.'

'Ugh!' Rowena said, but it worked. They went away happy and she vowed not to look at a single newspaper, sure that they would all embellish the facts.

Then, suddenly, there was only silence. Even Bruce had gone back to Ariana, and she was alone. To keep her mind off things she carried on with her work for Tom's chambers, uncertain if there would be any more forthcoming. If there wasn't, she would have to call on Miss Benson at the temp agency, because she needed the money.

One of the tabloids had offered her a very large sum of money to supply them with, they were pleased to call 'juicy details' but she had indignantly refused.

10

The one good thing about the whole nasty business was that it brought Rowena and Jude together again. Jude arrived at the house carrying a bunch of brightly-coloured daisies in one hand and a box of cream doughnuts in the other.

'I can't believe what I just read in the paper,' she gasped. 'Here, take these.' She thrust the gifts into Rowena's hands and stepped into the hall.

'So, tell me it all,' she said when they were sitting down.

Rowena was still greatly distressed by the experience and had already gone through the story several times, between explaining it to Bruce and the police, not to mention having reporters camped out on her doorstep.

She didn't really want to relive it all again, yet perhaps that was therapeutic.

If she talked about it often enough the horror might fade away, having lost its power to terrify her.

'I suppose it all started on the day the agency sent me to Tom's chambers to start there as a temp. Mark Collins had dropped in at the same time, and I imagine he got quite a shock when he saw me standing there. Poor Aunt Bettina was just about the same age as I am now when she died, and I'm told that we look very much alike.'

'I know. They put both your pictures in the paper. If I didn't know better I'd have thought you were twins.'

'Collins admitted that he was behind some nasty e-mails I was getting. He'd got off scot-free all these years, but meeting me must have got him worried. As you know, I was in the house when Aunt Bettina died and he probably thought I might be able to identify him.'

Jude was sceptical.

'After twenty-five years, and you just a toddler back then? Is that likely?'

'Hardly, but there was more to it than that, of course. I've been seeing his nephew, Tom Forrest, and I've been to several events at the family home. It must have seemed inevitable that as time went on Tom and I would share stories from our past. I would have explained about my horrible childhood experience. Tom could have mentioned that his uncle had once dated Aunt Bettina, and sooner or later somebody would have put two and two together.'

'So he hoped to frighten you off with his threats,' Jude said.

'Yes. He was often in and out of Tom's office, so it was easy for him to get my e-mail address from my personnel file. What he didn't bargain for was Bruce and me wanting to get to the bottom of the business of the letters. When I reported it to the police they said they couldn't do anything, and anyway they thought it was just crank stuff, you know? But once Collins learned that Bruce and I were snooping around he realised in his twisted mind that I had to be eliminated.'

'So what are you going to do about Tom, then?'

But Rowena didn't know how to answer that. She didn't want her lovely romance to end in such an ugly way.

'Let's talk about something else, shall we, Jude? What's new with you?'

'Well, there is this chap I met at the vegetable stall in the market . . . '

They were back on their old friendly footing. Rowena found that it was good to laugh again.

★ ★ ★

'I'm so sorry about all this, Rowena, more sorry than I can say.'

Tom's face crumpled, and she was afraid that he was about to burst into tears when he came to see her later that day.

'It's not your fault,' she said softly, placing a hand on his shoulder.

She would have liked to take him into her arms, but that hardly seemed appropriate, given the circumstances. He flung his arms wide in a gesture of hopelessness.

'I know, but I still feel responsible somehow. He is my uncle, after all. If I hadn't taken you out to Courtneys when Uncle Mark was there, it might never have resulted in all this trouble for you. When I think of what might have happened to you . . . ' He broke off with a sob.

'You forget that I met him when I came to your office that first day, as a temp,' she reminded him. 'That was just an unlucky chance, nothing to do with you at all. If I hadn't accepted that temp job when I did, our paths might never have crossed. And anyway, we can't hold ourselves responsible for what other people do.'

'At least I can tell you truthfully that I knew nothing about Uncle Mark's connection with your aunt,' Tom said, 'and of course you've never told me that there was a tragedy in your background, in any case. I must have been just a small boy when it took place, and naturally my parents didn't talk about the business in front of me.

'Now, Mother has admitted that she gave him a false alibi when the police were investigating Bettina's death. It wasn't that she was trying to cover up a crime, but she was absolutely sure that her brother could not have been involved and was just trying to extricate him from a rather sticky position. And apparently he had been staying with them that weekend in any case, so it wasn't a complete lie.

'She is absolutely horrified to think that you could have died, too, as a result of something she said so carelessly all those years ago. In fact, she can't stop crying about it. Poor Mother!'

Rowena didn't feel a lot of sympathy towards Mrs Forrest. If Mark had killed once, he could kill again, and she herself was proof of that. The woman had had no business making false statements to the police.

She did, however, believe that what Tom said was true, that his mother was misguided rather than actively trying to prevent the police from solving Bettina's murder.

'So as things go,' Tom said sadly, 'I don't see how we can continue with our relationship, do you? I love you, Rowena, and I'd hoped that you'd agree to marry me. In fact, I had it all planned. I meant to propose to you after the hunt ball next month. I'd even been to the jewellery shop and picked out a ring, in case you said yes.'

He gulped. 'But how could we ever be happy, with this terrible thing between us? The plain fact of the matter is that my uncle murdered your aunt and nothing can alter that.'

'I suppose you're right,' she told him, experiencing a feeling of sadness for what might have been. 'I think it would hurt my father dreadfully if our two families formed a bond. Bettina was his only sister, and he's never really got over her death.'

And there was Mrs Forrest, too, Rowena thought. No matter what her brother had done, there would always be that blood tie between them. How could she look favourably upon a daughter-in-law who had been the innocent means of putting him in prison for the rest of his life?

'So that's it, then,' Tom muttered. He swept her into his arms and they clung together for a long moment, the tears flowing freely down their faces now. 'Perhaps, in a year or two, when all this has died down . . . '

But Rowena knew it could never be.

She wriggled free of his embrace and rushed out of the room, the door swinging shut behind her, closing on all their hopes and dreams.

★　★　★

Three days later, Rowena finished her work on Morgan Evans' manuscript and prepared to take it back to his home. So many chapters in her life were coming to a close, it seemed.

Her mother, horrified to hear what had happened with Mark Collins, had offered to fly to England to be with her daughter. When Rowena assured her that it wasn't necessary, she had repeated her usual invitation to come for an Australian holiday.

Feeling rather fragile after all she had been through, Rowena was tempted to agree. In fact, might it not be best to put the house on the market and go abroad for good? The thought of all that sunshine and lovely beaches was wonderful.

She jumped when the doorbell rang, then had to remind herself that she was quite safe. Mark Collins was locked away where he couldn't get at her. She flung the door open to admit Bruce, who was standing on the step surrounded by suitcases and bulging bin bags.

'Can I come in, love?'

'What's all this, then?' She prodded the nearest bag with her toe.

'If you let me in I'll explain,' he grunted, picking up the larger of the two cases.

'The thing is,' he said hesitantly, when they were sitting at the kitchen table, drinking coffee, 'I've finally realised what a fool I've been. When I saw Collins standing over you like that I knew how devastated I'd be if anything ever happened to you.'

'The shock of the moment,' she commented.

'It wasn't just that, love. It made me see something I hadn't wanted to face before. I've never stopped loving you, Row. This thing with Ariana was just a sort of madness. I can't explain it. I seemed to be two people at the same time. One of me loved you, and the other who couldn't resist what the other woman had to offer.'

Rowena was silent. She didn't want to listen to a litany of Ariana's charms. As far as she was concerned the girl was a predatory female, who cared for nothing but her own desires. She became aware that Bruce was looking at her intently.

'So I was wondering, Row. Can you

ever forgive me? Do you think you can find it in your heart to take me back?'

He looks like a puppy who has been caught chewing the rug, Rowena thought. What should she tell him?

When he first walked out on her she would have given anything to hear him say those things, but now? She had been through so much and the old Rowena seemed like another person.

On the other hand, during all their recent expeditions they had fallen back into their old, comfortable relationship, as if they had never really been apart. Did she really want to throw all that away?

'What about Ariana?' she asked. Not that she cared, but it would be nice to know exactly where the girl fitted into the picture now.

'We had an almighty bust-up and she's gone for good,' Bruce admitted.

He seemed to think that made everything all right, Rowena thought. That being the case, she wasn't about to let him off lightly.

'I see. So you've come crawling back to me, have you? Charming!'

'It's not like that at all,' he protested. 'I told her I'd made a mistake and wanted to come back to you. She flared up and told me to go back to my boring wife, if that was what I wanted, and said she was going back to London where all the men weren't bogged down in domesticity. Something of an exaggeration, I felt.'

'Undoubtedly.'

'Well, come on, Rowena, what else do you want me to say? I know I've acted like a heel, but I've come back, cap in hand, to admit my mistake. I love you, I've always loved you, and I'll make it up to you, I promise I will. We've had too many good years between us before this happened. Are we going to let that count for nothing?'

Rowena knew what Jude would say.

'He had his chance and he blew it. Kick him out, girl. Who needs a rat like that?'

But what Jude would never understand was that she loved Bruce with all his failings, and was willing to give him a second chance.

'Perhaps we might give it a try,' she said cautiously. 'You can stay — in the spare room for now. We'll take it from there a day at a time and see how it works out.'

With a jubilant shout he picked her up and whirled her around, then, having carefully set her back on her feet he picked up his belongings and raced upstairs with them.

Smiling, Rowena watched him go. Getting back to their former secure footing would not be easy, but she was prepared to give it a try. The fact that she had never stopped loving her husband, even while she was dating Tom Forrest, would help them as they attempted to find their way back to the loving relationship that was rightfully theirs. She had come out of the shadows at last.

We do hope that you have enjoyed reading this large print book.

Did you know that all of our titles are available for purchase?

We publish a wide range of high quality large print books including:
Romances, Mysteries, Classics
General Fiction
Non Fiction and Westerns

Special interest titles available in large print are:
The Little Oxford Dictionary
Music Book, Song Book
Hymn Book, Service Book

Also available from us courtesy of Oxford University Press:
Young Readers' Dictionary
(large print edition)
Young Readers' Thesaurus
(large print edition)

For further information or a free brochure, please contact us at:
Ulverscroft Large Print Books Ltd.,
The Green, Bradgate Road, Anstey,
Leicester, LE7 7FU, England.
Tel: (00 44) 0116 236 4325
Fax: (00 44) 0116 234 0205